PANTHEON BOOKS NEW YORK

SiSTER CRA

SiSTER
CRAZY

Emma Richler

All rights reserved under International and Pan-American Copyright Conventions. Published in the United States by Pantheon Books, a division of Random House, Inc., New York, and simultaneously in Canada by Random House of Canada Limited, Toronto.

Pantheon Books and colophon are registered
trademarks of Random House, Inc.

Grateful acknowledgment is made to Sony/**ATV Music Publishing LLC** for permission to reprint lyrics from *Goldfinger* by John Barry, Leslie Bricusse, and Anthony Newley. Copyright © 1964 by Sony/ATV Songs LLC (renewed). All rights administered by Sony/ATV Music Publishing, 8 Music Square West, Nashville, TN 37203. All rights reserved. Reprinted by permission of Sony/ATV Music Publishing LLC.

Library of Congress Cataloging-in-Publication Data

Richler, Emma, 1961–
Sister crazy / Emma Richler.
p. cm.
ISBN 0-375-42108-4
1. Brothers and sisters—Fiction. 2. Young women—Fiction.
3. England—Fiction. 4. Canada—Fiction. I. Title.

PR6068.I249 S57 2001
823′.92—dc21   00-049188

www.pantheonbooks.com

Book design by Johanna S. Roebas

Printed in the United States of America
First Edition
2 4 6 8 9 7 5 3 1

FOR MY MOTHER AND MY FATHER
AND FOR BOB GOTTLIEB

.

CONTENTS

Talking Man   3

Angels' Share   22

Party Spirit   46

Running Time   76

Sister Crazy   104

Perilous Boy   135

No Time   174

SiSTER CRAZY

TALKING MAN

In the elaborate Action Man games I played with my brother Jude, games sometimes lasting for days, interrupted only for school, mealtimes, and homework, and involving complex missions, actual trenches, and tiny fireworks, there would be the occasional real casualty. A casualty might suffer a scary burn and get earth in its joints. At the end of a raid, he would be found in a heap with his foot some distance from his body, yes, dead with his boots on. This was always Talking Man. He was the brilliant Nazi officer, foiled again, the blithe stormtrooper just following orders or the double agent committing his final betrayal.

I was nine years old, and I had a sneaking admiration for the German uniform. I liked the tunic nipped in at the waist, the slim lapels, the rakish jodhpurs, the high boots, and the helmet which was a tidy compromise between the austerity of the Russian one and the sheer blowsiness of the American. And yet, we shuddered to dress our top men in this uniform; we only had it for the sake of verisimilitude. It gave us an over the shoulder feeling—is anybody watching?—to put a man in it. We only did so when we had pretty hard knocks in mind for the wearer. Talking Man wore it a lot.

In the days before soft boots with delicate laces that you could actually thread through eyelets, Talking Man had a pair of hard tight boots and changing them one day, I pulled his foot off too. With one of my favorite guys, this would have induced tears in me, and a desperate oh no feeling, but when it happened to Talking Man, I felt a shady satisfaction.

What did I have against him? Of all my men, I remember him most clearly, perhaps for the willful neglect I inflicted on his person as well as for a certain poignancy he represents for me to this day and which I am only now beginning to grasp.

I had acquired him through the Action Man reward system. With each purchase of an item from the Action Man directory, you were awarded stars in proportion to its value. For instance, a complete uniform—British Army Officer, German Stormtrooper, Alpine Commando, etc.—earned you maybe five stars. Whereas something from the Quartermaster's stores—a flare gun and radio unit; a detonator, coil of wire, and dynamite; a mess kit; a map case and binoculars—only afforded you one or two. When you had collected twenty-one stars you won a free Action Man. A free Action Man! I chose Talking Man, who was an innovation at the time. My heart sank when I saw him. On the box, things looked good. There was an actual-size painting of a soldier on it, dressed in an

RAF officer's uniform, his mouth ajar in mid-speech; he was clearly caught up in some grave moment and the words would be jaunty and ironic. I could tell he was a man used to self-sacrifice—ferociously brave, romantic at home, amusing and generous in the mess. In my memory, he resembled Sean Connery. It was not seemly to open the box in the shop, and I was too excited, having actually exchanged twenty-one cardboard stars for a whole man, to expect deception. But they really ought to have shown Talking Man naked on the packaging. A small picture of his torso would have been enough. I was simply not prepared for the facts. His chest was a mess of perforations, like grotesquely enlarged pores. I have ever since been disgusted by displays of regular perforations such as honeycombs or Band-Aids, the raised papillae of a burnt tongue, a pig's snout, moon craters, the magnified hair follicles in a razor ad, subway grates, cheese graters, the graininess of a blown-up photograph, aeration holes in a new lawn, the skin of a plucked chicken, the little holes on the surface of perfectly cooked rice. A plastic ring dangled from the middle of his back, below the shoulder blades, and attached to the ring was a long flesh-colored string that coiled within the hollow of his perforated chest, an intestinal rope, a terrible worm. Otherwise, Talking Man's features were regular, identical to all other Action Men, ones without stigmata, ones with minds of their own and no ready-made speech. And Talking Man's speech was simply insulting. How could his two or three uninspired phrases suit all occasions? I don't actually remember the few sentences in his repertoire, but they were of this ilk. "ATTENTION! FIRE DOWN BELOW! COVER ME! ALL HANDS ON DECK! ENEMY AIRCRAFT!" That sort of thing. And if any of these phrases came in handy, how would you know you'd hit on the right one? Even worse, this burst of speech was preceded by the noise of the cord uncoiling, followed by a shuffle and crackle of interference like announcements in a train station. Why couldn't he sound just a bit like Richard Burton in *The Desert Rats* or Jack Hawkins in *The Cruel Sea?* Instead, Talking Man might have been on drugs, or merely a simpleton. He never paused for thought. He did not experience doubt or pain or emotional stumbles of any kind. He just blurted out commands like a madman, all out delirium was a shot away. Then the military hospital— Northfield perhaps, near Birmingham—where he is deemed LMF. Lacking Moral Fibre. There he hides under beds and calls out in sleep to dead men, friends and enemies.

I expressed my contempt for Talking Man in small ways, quite apart from having him career headlong into ambushes and walk over landmines. When we went on our family summer holiday in Connemara, I left him behind. When Jude and I made undies and little vests out of old socks for our men, Talking Man had only bare skin next to his scratchy uniform. Action Man™ designed lovely long socks as part of their new sports line, and Jude and I saved them for our best men. Jude even made little garters out of black elastic. Not for Talking Man, however, the comfort of a warm knee sock. His feet were always bare, in hard boots. Or rather, his foot was always bare, in a hard boot.

I found the new sports line irksome. A booklet was available in the toy shops, and in it were colored illustrations of Action Man dribbling the ball, mid scissors kick, tackling, making a save, and kitted out in the colors of the most famous English clubs of the day: Arsenal, Liverpool, West Ham, Spurs. I could not reconcile the figure of my fighting World War II man and this frivolous sporting type. If at least they had been big shorts, like those of the thirties and forties, then I could work with the idea: our men are taking time out, on an RAF base, say, dispelling tension between raids, playing football with real yearning and abandon, expressing their comradeship in war, and nostalgia for their curtailed youth. They are very deft at the game, in an unfussy, self-effacing way. They are unselfish, laying off passes for men recovering from disfigurement, or men whose wives had perished in air raids or who were unfaithful to them, unable to live in fear of the awful telegram.

"What is it, Alice? Bad news?"

For my men, praise in the course of a match would be generously deflected by jovial cracks at their own expense. Talking Man, of course, never played in these matches, even before his crippling accident, when he was sidelined due to craziness. I had seen some old footage taken by psychiatrists in one of the military hospitals, the Royal Victoria or Craiglockhart, set up during the '14–'18 scrap, a film showing the funny walks of shell-shocked men. Names were given to all the funny walks, dancing gait, slippery footing on ice gait, fighting the wind gait, climbing up a mountain gait. Talking Man had dancing gait. He was a bad case and beyond rescue.

On the rare occasions when Jude and I allowed a guest player, one not to be trusted with our finest men, he would get Talking Man. Like our brother Ben, who was keen to steer our games into bizarre realms.

"You know that many Nazi officers belonged to occult societies?"

Stony looks from Jude and me.

"Well let's say they stumble on these caves where satanic rituals are taking place and . . ."

Usually we just let Ben handle the fireworks for the true to life trench warfare, until, that is, he managed to melt the neck of one of Jude's leading men.

"Well done," Jude said aggressively.

"Yeah," I added, "well done."

"But it's so realistic!" said Ben, eyes flashing. "What if *all* the men had some kind of injury and . . ."

Although Ben was our big brother, and in general we flocked to him for entertainment, he was terrible at Action Man. So we fell on a plan. If he were passing, Jude and I would act so engrossed in our game we didn't notice him; it would be a faux pas on his part to ask to join in. This rankled with me a little and I felt hot in the pit of my stomach and would have an urge to leap up and chase after him, offering up my best man, the one with dark hair and an excellent physique, by which I mean, since all Action Men have the same build, that his joints were neither unyielding nor loose. He could wield a machine gun one-handed; he could crouch in a stealthy manner for any length of time without slipping, no worries. I saved up and bought him the beautiful uniform of the Royal Horse Guards, a ceremonial kit intended for dress occasions such as bashing off on parade or receiving honors, etc. Because our men were mostly engaged in missions of serious strategic complexity requiring them to slither through undergrowth, duck into abandoned cellars, scale dizzying heights and examine maps in hellish conditions, the Guards uniform was largely unworn. Until the time, that is, when Jude found pursuits that did not involve me so much anymore.

When Jude went off with his boyfriends, it was harder and harder for him to argue for my presence without calling a lot of attention to himself. He had a laconic demeanor and a fiercely protective nature and he needed all parties to be at ease, so the best solution for him at the time was to leave me out.

Once, I was allowed to play with Jude and his friend Michael, who was lean and silent and glamorous with ruffled fair hair. But during this game we were all a little stifled. It was an experiment doomed to failure, a one-off occasion. At home the next day, after school, Jude mumbled a message to me.

"Michael says he enjoyed your presence," he said, passing me on the stairs.

"My what?"

"YOUR PRESENCE!" Jude repeated crossly.

"Oh. Great." I didn't know what Michael meant about presents (what presents?) but I was aroused by this communication from him and I felt shifty, too, as if I had betrayed Jude somehow. In my mind, I thought I saw Jude take one more step away from me. The curtain was dropping on this episode of our oneness and so I let him go. But I refused to see it as desertion. No. We are SOE (Special Operations Executive). As natural leaders, we had to be split up. In Occupied France, two separate targets, and for our own protection, two secret routes. Would we survive? Will we meet again?

"See you at the Ritz in springtime. Make mine a champagne cocktail."

More and more, then, I took the white breeches and the scarlet coat of the Royal Horse Guards off the little coat hangers that Jude and I had fashioned from copper wire and I dressed my man in it. I dressed him by degrees and with languorous gestures I can only think of now as intimations of sensuality.

My man liked to read whenever he was not engaged on the field of battle. Jude and I made books for our men by cutting up the spines of comics. You could get about eighteen books from the spine of one single *Victor* comic, for example. A good haul. Then you designed a cover and stuck it on. *The Last Enemy, All Quiet on the Western Front.* Maybe even *Wuthering Heights.* My man always had a book in his rucksack. He reminded me of my parents' friend Rex, a famous cinematographer who dressed in jeans and white T-shirts and blue cashmere sweaters. He had very elegant features and a band of flowing white hair around his otherwise bald head. He had a reckless streak and a languid demeanor. He answered yes or no to most queries in a languid fashion. He was not expansive. Jude and I spotted a German Luger in his house. The real thing. We were in awe. We asked Rex about it in hopeful and timid voices. He was elusive, which was downright glamorous to us, he came to me and held my long fair hair in his gentle grasp and asked airily, to no one visible, "Does anyone have a pair of scissors?"

Playing alone, I liked to sit my man on the edge of his khaki bunk, a book splayed and held open by the hand with the pointing index finger and thumb. "Death," he reads in *The Last Enemy,* his favorite, "should be given the setting it deserves; it should never be a pettiness; and for the fighter pilot it never can be." My man would be half-dressed in this moment of repose, wearing only his tall black Horse Guards boots with the silver spurs and his close-fitting white breeches with the lovely braces. I angled his head so he seemed to glance thoughtfully somewhere in the middle distance, which is an expression I had caught in my mother when she was reading. I tried to read this way myself, but lost a lot of time being distracted by other things out there in the middle distance and then trying to find my place on the page again. Never mind. It was out of duress that I played alone, but I was suddenly able to observe my man's physiognomy at leisure and to allow him those moments when he could assume off-guard qualities, quite literally. The sight of him with the delicate white braces criss-crossing his slim, muscular, hairless chest gave me a distinct pleasure. The contrast of extreme formality with the undress of reverie lent him an air of vulnerability. Vanity was a foreign thing to my man. If pressed, he might own up to gratitude for his good looks, but he never traded them for favors, oh no.

Something thrown up in the drift of Jude's wake, in his flow toward other people, was a new game we tried out together once or twice, a game involving my sister's Barbie, a game that held him for a little while longer.

Barbie could not go far with us without overstretching the boundaries of truth. She could be a sort of Mary Ure in *The Guns of Navarone*, a commando with useful feminine wiles and a gift for disguise and languages. Or a nurse maybe, caught up in a daring mission and proving invaluable, Sylvia Syms in *Ice Cold in Alex*. An obvious choice was Barbie as French Resistance fighter, headstrong and relentless, going boldly where no French woman has gone before. There was also the aristocratic English girl, a master code-breaker for MI6. Women with no spare time on their hands, no time for dates, which is what I suspected Jude craved above all. And so most often, Barbie was a glamorous double agent, passing secrets to her man as he breezed through Occupied Paris, always an occasion for champagne and smuggled Russian caviar. Silk stockings and Virginia tobacco, rare as golddust, were regular features.

Something happened. I became tongue-tied and short of breath. My dramatic abilities failed me. My temples hurt. Later in life, in cases of sudden awareness on dates (Oh, I thought I liked you), when the urge to escape the sexual showdown is sharp as a fire alarm and you want to flee in cartoon time—in the first frame, one arm in a sleeve and coattails flapping; in the next, home in bed, reading a Tintin book—I would remember this atmosphere of disquiet and asphyxiation that came upon me with Jude and my sister's Barbie. All I could do was stall.

"Just a minute here! How did your man enter Paris? Subterfuge? Fake passport? Is my man with him? Shouldn't he be? What mission is this? Shouldn't he be in a hurry?"

Even episodes with the French Resistance girl of the one-track mind (*Vive la France!*) degenerated into dates. Crawling through darkened forests, sabotaging power lines, setting booby traps and gathering secret munitions drops, Jude's man still managed to suggest dinner and dancing. So I revolted. I started to get silly as the walls of illusion came tumbling down, exposing the scene for what it was—sex—and Jude either got slaphappy along with me or stalked off in a fury. End of game. The second thing I would do was dry up, a startled and exhausted actor. I dithered and looked spacey and we would have to pause for peanut butter sandwiches. The third ploy was to say quietly, in a fit of uncommon generosity, "We should invite Harriet to play, you know. We shouldn't take her Barbie and not ask her to play." End of game. Harriet was only six and extremely hopeless at serious games; even Gus could do better, and he was a baby still, two years old and not ready for war. So finally, in the absence of Jude, it was my fate to learn to play with her.

Explaining any new discipline to Harriet, you had to tether her to reality by introducing minor rules and practicalities, although never too many at once or she was liable to break off in the middle of things and start dancing to an unidentifiable tune of her own. Looking for Harriet, calling her to supper, say, or for school, you were likely to find her skipping around in the garden, a fairy on a happy day out in the ether. Harriet's fierce whim was for collecting stuffed animals of all sizes, chiefly lambs and bird life, especially chicks, as well as a few bears and rabbits.

I gave her the lowdown on World War II. She needed to know the rugged truth in order to play, although she would dwell on the least vital points.

"Yes but . . ." Then the dancing around began, inducing wide-eyed exasperation in me. If I gave up, she wailed.

"I want to play! I *want* to!"

Oh God.

I rehearsed her, but it was no good; before too long, there would be Barbie with her deranged look, handing out minute teacups containing drops of water to my Action Men, surrounded by the beasts of the field.

This was not like playing with Jude. Harriet didn't really need me at all. I even left her with Talking Man, making out that this was something of a sacrifice, as if he were my favorite man. I watched her for a short while as I edged my way out. She was squeezing Talking Man into some of Barbie's more loose-fitting garments—Transvestite Man now—and submitting him to minor indignities such as talking to animals, dancing and singing in his flounces, and preparing refreshments for a lot of chicks and little lambs. Meanwhile Barbie preened quietly, looking on from the sidelines, happy in a sort of maniacal way, grateful for the company. My sister even pulled Talking Man's ring, suffering a jolt of alarm at the blurt of officious speech that issued forth. Harriet was simply not used to gruff commands except in fun, in our dad's voice, say, the monster one he used when chasing her, stomping around the house with his hair all mussed. She did not like Talking Man's voice at all. I saw her give him a startled look, then a cold one, as she went about wiping the event from her memory. She was really good at that, breezing on by things she didn't like.

Jude and I had discovered one use for Talking Man's urgent monotone. It was easy to induce dementia in him by making incomplete jerks of varying lengths on his vocal cord so that he'd only speak fragments of his stock phrases, which you could interrupt at random until he sounded ready for the white jacket with the long sleeves tied up at the back. This game had limited amusement value and Jude and I indulged in it only when flagging and war-weary and vulnerable to hilarity. I yanked Talking Man's ring pull in jerks. "ATT-" . . . "-DOWN BE-" . . . "-HANDS ON-" etc. We started yelling at each other.

"Make me a peanut butter sandwich now!"

"Have you done your homework!"

"No!"

"What's for supper!"

"Ask Mummy!"

"Ask her yourself!"

"Dismissed!"

"Okay!"

"Shut up!"

Jude and I are only fifteen months apart, and in spite of ourselves, I guess, we have a twin mentality, which time and distance cannot take away. Those are the facts. Jude likes to say from time to time, "You were a mistake. You were not supposed to happen."

Considering I am not my parents' last born, I do not take this seriously. I came too soon, okay, I can deal with that. I let him have his fun, though. I let him think I am slightly alarmed, but I am not. I have doubts about many things but I am absolutely sure that I was born out of love, despite my affinity for wartime.

Jude and I were steeped in World War II, although we were born some fifteen years after it ended. Knowing about the war gave me a sense of distinction, as if I, too, had suffered and overcome, emerging with my own badge of courage. I knew it as a black-and-white time, a place of shadows and relentless drizzle and austerity, of necessary violence and amazing resilience, a world in bold focus. I was there and Jude was with me.

Now I am in the room full of clocks where the voice calls out, WAKE UP! MOVE ALONG! HONEY, IT'S TIME!

I look at Action Man in 1999 and connect only with the name; everything else is strange to me. The packaging screams its gaudy colors of fire and blood and tropical locations, having all to do with fantasy and nothing to do with the high stakes and redemption that we played for. Even the man looks different, rubbery and matte-finished, with a sunbed tint and the vain five-o'clock shadow of the gigolo, not of the man suffering sleep deprivation and high anxiety. The men are marketed now under different names, clamorous titles of hollow intensity: "THE BOWMAN!" "ROLLER EXTREME!" "AGENT 2000!" "SKY DIVER!" "CRIMEBUSTER!" "OPERATION JUNGLE!" "SURF RESCUE!" They have special vehicles: GYRO COPTER, and POLAR MISSION TURBO 4×4 fires as you drive! Mission cards are included and a disclaimer is written on the boxes, in more demure print: "Action Man™ does not identify with any known living person."

Picking up these packages in the toy department, pretending to be shopping for a son or nephew, I feel a little scornful and superior. But what do I know about war? I crave the old me. Now I miss things like decision and certainty, beginnings and endings. In grown-up life, there are few demarcations. It is a great battlefield with constantly shifting fronts, that's how I see it. Where, for instance, do I end and Jude begin? When does childhood end? No one ever said anything.

We were all corralled by our parents into watching a Steinbeck dramatization one evening in extreme youth, probably *The Grapes of Wrath,* and we lay on the floor in front of the TV stunned, literally, by the Great Depression. Everyone in the drama wandered about wearing skimpy, threadbare clothing and droopy expressions, speaking in defeated monotones, going to sleep on hard floors after a meal of one bulbous parsnip. The mother woke up the children at five in the morning, nudging them into readiness for another cotton-picking day. "Honey," she said to each one of them, followed by a gloomy pause, "it's time." This scene happened at least eight times in the drama. My sister and I were sniggering wrecks by bedtime, hardly able to negotiate the stairs for hilarity. Waking up for school from then on we would say to each other, "Honey." BIG PAUSE. "It's time."

1914–1918. 1939–1945. I marveled at a world at war and I could not fathom anything but conflict, beginning and ending with shocking decisiveness. I could not imagine the home front. I could not picture any casual activity at all. Surely shops were empty and gardens overgrown and any person without a gun in foreign fields could only stand on a rooftop with a helmet and torch or sit fretting by a window in a darkened house, straggly-haired and wide-eyed with grief and worry but steeled by virtue. Films, therefore, that showed the truth—that is, some semblance of normality going on at home while battles raged—were downright distracting to me.

"I don't understand, Jude. Why are they in a restaurant? Jude, why is she laughing? Jude, when is this happening? What is going on?"

Jude did not always answer me, at least not right away. Sometimes he would answer me several hours from the time I asked a question, or even the next day. I was used to this. That time, for instance, Jude came back from one of his Robin Hood sorties to the sweetshop. Jude stole sweets with his friends and shared them out at home. I found this diligent generosity poignant. So Jude said to me suddenly, passing me a red fruit gum, my favorite, "He is on leave. He is home recovering from a wound. She is hysterical due to war. It is not really a happy laugh."

"Oh," I said. "Okay, thanks."

I always knew which conversation he was resurrecting. I just did.

We were leaving home, where we were born, and moving to my dad's country, where he was born, and we were sailing there on the SS *Pushkin*. We packed. Action Man packed. Jude decided we had to be a bit ruthless and thin out the equipment and the wardrobe.

17

We could not take everything with us, so we made packages to sell to Jude's friends. I did not know any girls in my convent school who played with Action Man; it was not a suitable marketplace. Besides, a convent does not encourage the entrepreneur.

Jude and I took shirt cardboard from Dad's drawer and sewed on items of uniform, ironing the clothing first of all. The tunic would be displayed just so, one arm flung out and the other laid across the chest at an angle. The trousers we attached by two stitches and set in profile, the waistband tucked under the skirting of the jacket. Jude had stronger fingers and he stitched the shoes below the trousers and attached the hat or helmet above the jacket collar, where the head would be. The accessories were arrayed to one side, under the outstretched arm: gun, belt, pouch, water bottle, etc. There might be extras of our own design such as a book, a hanger, real braces with snaps, undies, or a vest. This gave the package real distinction. Jude then wrote out prices—£1.10, £1.70, etc.—and some slogan in eye-catching lettering; "MAKE YOUR MAN THE SMARTEST IN THE NEIGHBORHOOD!" for instance. He even supplied stars at the bottom of the cardboard display sheet which you could collect and redeem against further purchases.

"But Jude," I said, "what will we give away? We are taking the rest of the stuff with us. And we won't even be here." I had visions of irate schoolboys clutching stars and yelling our names accusingly, forcing their way through a crowded quayside where the SS *Pushkin* was docked. But Jude waved all objections aside simply by looking at me with his slow gaze and not answering. In a finishing touch, we covered each cardboard sheet with cellophane and Jude took the packages with him to school.

I had an idea we could sell Talking Man. He could be marketed as a sort of special business extra—Casualty Man. Because mostly you would not want to sacrifice your best men in a scene with a lot of extras, and it was realistic to have strewn bodies, it would be a bonus to have a Casualty Man just for the sake of verisimilitude. I said we could advertise Talking Man right away as the FREE GIFT with stars, which would solve that little deception in one stroke. People would know what they were aiming for and it might even quicken sales.

Jude said, "I'll think about it." This meant no.

What should I do with Talking Man? He was too pathetic to take with us and to me he suggested unmarked graves and dead men in transport ships, only recognizable thanks to identity bracelets. I thought of dockside welcoming committees, wailing women and stoical fathers with bleeding hearts and stone-cold corpses under shrouds on stretchers. And so I left Talking Man behind, accidentally on purpose. Forgive me, Talking Man, Ugly Man, One Foot, Enemy, Traitor, LMF Man, Shell-Shock Man, Missing in Action Man, Transvestite Man, Misfit Man—over and out. Au revoir, old thing; cheerio, farewell, goodbyee.

Jude is a foreign correspondent now.

I had a dream recently that I was on assignment with him. Real Action Men now. We are running in a crouched position in the water, along the edge of a river. We have automatic rifles. I am thrilled and I feel safe. My brother is a war correspondent and he cannot be killed. He fires at snipers while we scamper along but misses intentionally, signaling to them merrily. I am charged with pride. I glance back at the snipers and see in their faces a calculated pretense of gratitude. They do not care that Jude spared them and suddenly I know they will shoot him. I need to warn him but it is too late. They shoot me. My face is falling into the water, I fall slowly. Oh-oh. My back feels hot.

"Jude, am I hit? Jude, am I?"

Jude says, "No. No."

"Oh, I think so," I say, smiling a little. "Yes, I think so, Jude."

I am aware of the coming oblivion, the terrible loneliness of death, and I see this reflected in Jude's eyes as I fall into his arms. I know we are too far from help. His look is grave, wary; he is speechless with impending loss, although his actions are careful and practical, plugging the exit wounds with his fingers, supporting my drooping head, as if in not recognizing death rushing toward me, he can prevent even this.

Jude has a knack for choosing to investigate a place that is about to be torn apart by hostilities, a place rife with fanatics and con men. He has a tendency to stand up in press conferences and ask provocative questions in the most unassuming way, with gravity and charm. He is probing and brave and he rallies people to him. I hope his charm will protect him. I hope his charm is bulletproof.

I watch him walk away from me after sharing a drink on the eve of an assignment and I note the loping strides he takes, even though he is not a tall man. I note his head tilted to one side slightly, tilted in thought, and that he moves away at a pace never faster than ambling, although I know his bags are not packed and he leaves in less than three hours. To my surprise, I think of Talking Man. I imagine I hold the ring pull of his speech cord and the farther Jude walks from me, the longer and tauter the cord becomes. I must hold tight because if I let go, Jude will find himself,

I envisage, rooted to the spot, and with the release of the tension he will feel real fear for once, and there will come from his mouth a vulnerable rush of speech, a babble of strange words, and he will be lost.

Wherever he is, and no matter what, even flying gunfire and so on, Jude calls me on the telephone when he is reporting from a war-torn place. Wherever he is. He might ask me a sporting question. How is my team doing? Who scored? He might send me on an errand. Please water my plants. Please call my office. Please prune the peony bush. He might describe the meal he just ate, his room, or some arresting vision he has seen in the strange place he is in. This time, though, I have not heard from him in twenty-three days. I wake up sometimes in the middle of the night. I am wide awake, my heart is hammering, my throat parched, my teeth aching from clamping my jaw shut in fitful sleep. I call out his name and I ask, "Where are you?" I say it a second time, more quietly, "Where are you?"

I am in the room full of clocks and now there is no voice, just ticking. It's okay. I'm holding tight, I won't let go.

ANGELS' SHARE

My dad is really grumpy now. It happened somewhere back on the road, sometime between his slouching into the driver's seat and the end of this fifteen-minute journey from our summer cottage to the next village. I don't know. Maybe he spotted Indians in the hills. Maybe he felt our little wagon train was under threat and we are far, far from any army outpost. Rescue is not likely. He won't say a thing about it, though, to my mother or to me, his sole passengers. He is a tight-lipped man. Being provider and protector is one devil of a job in a big country, I can see that.

It's a fine afternoon and the sky is a slaphappy blue but I wish there were a slight breeze, just enough to ruffle the leaves a little, enough to break up the menace of a still, hot day. I want to open the window but my dad would not like this, so I don't. If you open the window, the air conditioning in the car, one of the few features he knows how to operate without having to ask anyone, will not work properly. I would rather have real air play over my face, but I try not to think about it. I try not to feel tyrannized by air conditioning. We are nearly there. I hope I will not be sick. I feel hot and cold and somewhat nauseous and the tension level in the car is high, pressing on my temples, making my heart race. My mother is looking out of her window and she says something in febrile, purposeful tones. She is always ready to dispel gloom.

"I just saw the most beautiful bird!" she says, or something like that. We are nearly there. The Indians are on the warpath and this last stretch of road seems endless to me, fraught with danger. I am unarmed. Dad won't teach me how to use a gun because I am a girl and it is unseemly and he thinks I won't need it. He will protect me. I hope so.

I wish he'd say something. I wish I were a boy. Then maybe we would not be taking this sissy journey to the chemist for an herbal remedy for depression and my dad would not be so mad at me.

I could be Doc Holliday. That would be very good. I have a deadly disease and I deal with it in a manly way. I have no time for it. It does not diminish me. There will be no gauzy visions of angels, no lingering goodbyes. I retch and splutter grudgingly into squares of white linen. Goddamnit, there goes another hanky. Pitch it into the fireplace. Good shot.

My woman gives me that boring look, her eyes sparkling with fear and pity.

"Stop that! Get out! Leave me alone!"

I reach for the whisky and I don't bother with a glass. It is possible I drink too much. Never mind. As long as I can shoot straight. As long as I can stand up for my friends and walk an unswerving line to the O.K. Corral. On that day, I'll be wearing my finest, no fraying cuffs.

There's a knock on the door. Here comes Wyatt. He leans against the door and walks over to the bedside table and picks up my whisky bottle, meaning, this much already? It's only eleven A.M. We don't speak, though. Don't worry, Wyatt. I'll be there. He knows that. I cough.

"See a doctor."

"No doctors."

"Get some rest," he says, heading for the door.

Dad just spoke.

"What?" I say. "Sorry, what?"

"We are not going to any other shops. Just the chemist. I'll stay in the car. You have ten minutes."

I start singing in my head, the tune from the Sturges film *Gunfight at the O.K. Corral*. O-KAAAY . . . co—RAAL! O-KAAAY . . . co—RAAAAL! I almost sing it aloud. I want to, because it might make my dad laugh, but I worry that for once it won't, that he won't join in and I'll feel bad, worse than I do already. The song rises, then dies in my chest and I miss my chance and that's the hell of this thing, this sissy, crackpot, sneaky disease which is not okay, like consumption with its angry, show-off blood on wads of linen.

"Jem?"

"Yes?"

"Did you hear what I said?"

I can see Dad's eyes looking at me in the rearview mirror. He has wild brows and his eyes are narrowed, weather-beaten lines running from the corners toward his temples. He is a handsome man in an unruly way and he has a gunslinger's gaze. This comes from years of squinting into a high sun and into duststorms and sharp night winds. It comes from a perpetual state of wariness and the need to see around things and be ready at all times. Anything can happen but you must stay cool. You have to master the distant look and know how to forage the horizon for looming dangers such as wild beasts, Apaches, and other gunslingers with sharp, squinty vision who might be on your trail.

When my dad talks to me, the little muscles around his eyes bunch up, giving him that gunslinger look. I have the distinct sensation he is not having a good time having to make words, having to speak at all. It's the way he is and you have to get used to it. His vision is acute, he is the only one in the family who doesn't need glasses.

"We are not going to any other shops—just the chemist."

"Right." My dad looks at the road now.

I practice a gunslinger squint. I can see my reflection in the window, which I keep closed due to air conditioning, and my face is dappled with tree leaves and other passing things, but I can see my eyes. I look silly, because a gunfighter cannot wear glasses and look cool. A good cowboy does not wear specs. I think about those crazy glasses you have to look through at the optician's, your chin resting in a cup. They are like the periscope sights that a U-boat commander needs to spot enemy vessels. The optician slips different lenses into the apparatus with maddening speed and he keeps saying in bored tones, "Better or worse? Better or worse?" until I want to scream and I am so confused and pressured by him,

I stumble out with eyeglasses of magnifying strength. I can spot spiders several paving stones away, but people look spooky. No one should have to see in such gory detail.

Better or worse? I asked myself each time I was put on a new medication. New medications and higher and higher doses. Better or worse? I asked myself, my heart thudding, hallucinating kaleidoscopic visions, sweating through the chic French pyjamas I wore because I felt so cold, soaking my white linen sheets, bringing towels back to bed, scared and ashamed after vomiting into the toilet on the hour through the night. This is a good medication. In small doses it is not always therapeutic. It is definitely helping you and I think you should not keep going on and off it, says the doctor. It is working.

Okay. Cool.

Dad is looking at me again in the mirror. Now what? Nothing. He looks at me this way because he is not all that wild about me right now, the crazy, drugged-up daughter, and also because he is a cowboy and that is the way they look at people. I used to be a cowboy, too. Dad and me in the Wild West, stalking the main street, bringing home the vittles for Maw, not before sliding onto bar stools, our packages falling around our feet.

"What'll it be?"

"Mâcon-Villages," I say.

My dad nods and gestures with his eyes for me to repeat this to the barman. My dad does not like to speak French unless it is strictly called for.

"A glass of Mâcon blanc, please," I say.

My dad drinks single malt. Doubles with a splash on the side. He hunkers down over his drink and lights a thin cigar. Thin but not skinny. His eyes slide slowly to one side or upward as he checks

out the crowd, but his head hardly moves except for a slight raising of the chin, the better to draw on his cigar. We do not say
much.

I know some things my dad does not know. Or care about. For
instance, all Scotch malt whisky is produced in a pot still, a distil-
lation of barley. Starch in barley is converted to sugar by virtue of
a controlled germination, a process arrested in a peat kiln. Now
you have malt. Malt is ground into grist and mixed with hot water
in a mash tun, and the sweet liquid, the wort, is drawn off into a
fermenting vat. This is now the wash. The wash is distilled into
low wines and these are redistilled into raw whisky, the middle dis-
tillate with the foreshots and feints removed. It becomes Scotch
when it has aged in oak for a minimum of three years. Unblended
and the product of a single distillery, it is a single malt. These are
the basics.

My dad favors Highland malt although he wouldn't care to say
why. He could not even tell you he specifically likes Speyside
whisky. He would not want to discuss it much less hear about why
it is different from Islay malt. Okay.

Something else I want to tell my dad. When the whisky is maturing for eight, twelve, fifteen, seventeen, twenty-one years, what
this really means is the liquid is concentrating, breathing in the
sea and the river and the heather and iodine and breathing out
water, esters and alcohol into the atmosphere. In Cognac, the
French call this evaporation *la part des anges*. The angels' share.
I love this idea. I also think it is only fair, because they must have
to share a lot of worse things in the thinning ozone and I hope
there are a lot of angels gathering over the Highlands, especially
Speyside, over Islay and the Orkney Islands and Campbelton and
the Lowlands. I know they have cousins hovering over Cognac and

Ténarèze in Armagnac and the Vallée d'Auge, where calvados is made, even wherever the marc is distilled in the wine regions, Champagne and Burgundy. In Cognac, the wine warehouse where old cognac is stored is called *le paradis*. A lot of angels lurk there and I wish them well.

My dad tips back the last sip of malt. He is ready to go, although I have not finished my drink. That's okay. I have all my life to drink at my leisure and right now I am with my dad and these are good times and I want to stick with him, go when he goes, go where he goes. At heart, I am not the Doc at all, I am Joey and he is Shane and he is definitely the man to follow.

"Let's go. Finished?"

No. "Yup," I say, rising quickly. We saunter out.

I remember another time, another bar. Dad has Mum on one arm and me on the other. It is late and we are having a nightcap at the Ritz. I like this word "nightcap," putting a cap on the night, tipping your brim at the daytime. There goes another day. Let's call it a day.

Dad is a bit sloshed and it makes him merry and a bit unpredictable. I sense high jinks. A couple is leaving the Ritz bar as we approach it and they want to greet my dad but he has no time for them, he does not like these people. They begin to say something and there is a look that comes over them. Appeasement, ingratiation. My dad barks at them, "Ruff!" Just like a dog. His hair musses even more. Mum and I fight to quell hilarity. What my dad has done is the equivalent of reaching for his six-shooter, of fluttering his trigger fingers over the holster at his hip. He is a cowboy, don't they know that? We leave them in our wake, frozen with their mouths agape.

It is great being with my dad. These are good times I am look-ing back on. I wonder if they will come again soon. Some days, I doubt it. I just don't see it. Like today, on the way to find an herbal remedy for depression with my dad looking at me suspiciously in the mirror and me fighting the silverfish in my veins and the fero-cious urge to throw up all over his posh new car, which is littered, nevertheless, with Visa slips and tomato stalks and empty en-velopes. The man can't help it, he marks his territory out and I, today, these days, am the intruder. Get off my land. Come back when you are well, when you are a cowboy again and can roam with me. I don't know you now.

Do not cry, Jem, I say to myself. Come on now, do not be a baby. Do not be a girl.

Besides looking back on good times and trying to fathom them, I write my book in my head. It is a survival book, a book of rules. It won't be long but it will be very useful. Here is rule number one.

1. NEVER LEAVE YOUR GLASSES ON THE FLOOR.

I have discovered there is no loophole to this rule. Even if you say to yourself, okay, I have just set my specs on the floor. I see my-self do it, I etch it on my memory. No way I'll step on them or kick them across the floor. Then it happens. The phone rings and you jump right on top of them or you nap for a minute and shake awake suddenly and swivel your body off the sofa, landing your feet back on the floor. Right onto the specs, goddamnit. So that's rule number one. Never leave your glasses on the floor. Thank you.

2. NEVER LEAVE YOUR WINEGLASS ON THE FLOOR.

Same potential disasters as above.

When we left the bar that day with our shopping bags, my dad said, "Let's call home. Just in case. We don't want to have to go out again."

My dad has seen enough of the world and he has one vision in his mind. It is of a big sofa with a tomato snack by his side and a mess of newspapers all around him. Soon Mum will call out to him, Darling! Supper. Ah, the best moment of the day.

Right now, though, what my dad really wants to do is to chuckle over the fact we could not find truffle butter. When Mum wrote this down on our list he was gleeful. He thought this was hilarious and he was pretty determined to be right about this item not existing out there in the western world as he knows it. In the two places we tried, he made me ask for it, truffle butter being two words too girly for him to utter. At the first shop, he even waited outside, only coming in after it was clear my request had not been met. We laughed.

Before we get to lord it over Mum, my dad has to tackle the public-telephone situation.

"Jem," he says, serious now, "we'll try this one."

I sigh with anticipation. This will be fun.

He pushes on the door of the nearest booth, meeting resistance.

"Hey!" he says. There is a lot of resistance to my dad out there in the physical world. He figures the door business out and drops a coin in after scanning all the instructions wildly and deciding to ignore them. The phone machine swallows the coin and that's it, no joy. He thumps the machine about three times.

"Goddamnit!"

I reach in and press coin return and check the slot. "Let's try another one, Dad."

In the next booth, I can see through the window that he is doing a lot of crazy thumping and is prepared to jump ship. I open the door and reach through the mayhem to press the button under the coin slot, right near the instruction that reads, Press after each coin entered.

"Oh," he says and dials home. He looks back at me in exhilaration. He is about to reveal to Mum the sheer folly of her shopping mission. He can't wait.

3. GIVE INSTRUCTIONS A CHANCE.

Instructions are sometimes written for those with below expected mental capacity. For instance, on a package of plasters, I read in step two, "Apply plaster." On a tube of skin salve, "Apply a little cream." Well, why not? But some instructions are useful. On page one of my video-machine booklet, it says, "To reduce the risk of fire or shock hazard, do not expose this equipment to rain." I do not know who would watch their TV and video out in a field when it is raining but never mind, this is important information for those people who are tempted. "Do not exceed the stated dose." This, I find, is important news. I remember a time, in dark days, when I was not Joey or the Doc and I was riding in cars on the way to health shops in search of herbal remedies for depression, yes, I remember a time when this was a vital instruction that I intended to ignore. I wanted very much to largely exceed the stated dose. This was exactly my plan before I decided that I did not want anyone else to wear my agnès b. clothes and that I wanted to finish the novel I was reading but mostly the look I imagined on Mum's face at the sight of my grim and excessively dosed self on the carpet was too unbearable to contemplate. So I put off my date with death. It was a postponement I had in mind, that is all.

Strange though, I thought, my dad will be okay. He'll get over it. When you are a cowboy, you see all kinds of things, sudden death and gruesome moments of all varieties, and you just have to endure it all. People depend on you to do this.

"I'll be darned," a cowboy might say over some gory reality, pulling a fresh cheroot from a shirt pocket, maybe tipping his hat back for a second, swiping the heat from his brow. "I'll be darned. Lookee here."

When my dad finished his gleeful phone call that day, we chuckled for some time. He bought flowers, white ones which Mum especially likes, on the way home.

"This'll keep her busy," he cracks, in that Wild West fashion. The fact is, he is crazy about her.

He walks with me. I call it a saunter. My dad has a steadfast, ruminative walk. He takes command of his space. I only ever saw him hurry once, when Mum broke her wrist badly, gardening on a slope, when she was in a state of turmoil over his moodiness. It was a terrible break and he had to drive a long way to a good hospital and I was there too, sitting in the back of the car with my broken-up mother who was making cheery comments to keep us calm, despite a lower arm that looked like bits of snapped kindling. My dad's back, I could see, was dark with sweat and he was leaning into the steering wheel as if he could impel the vehicle onward this way, or maybe speed us into a happier time zone, a place without injury.

4. NEVER GARDEN ON A SLOPE WHEN IN A STATE OF TUR-MOIL.

My dad walks with me. He is gripping my neck, loosely he thinks, in a manner suggesting fellowship and affection. It feels good although his grip is a little like those sinks in the hair salon, designed to hold your head in place but actually inviting disaster, such as permanent spinal injury and wholesale numbing of the nervous system. But I like walking with my dad this way. The world is ours. No one would dare pull a gun on us, nor even call out a careless remark. Everyone wants to be us, I can tell.

But who is this man, I cannot help asking myself, who believes that a thump will make a thing function? My dad is a pummeler of dashboards, a boxer of boilers, a rattler of fax machines, telephones, turnstiles and parking meters, a walloper of drinks dispensers, a slapper of remote controls. He is the man you see stabbing a lift button eight or nine times. He is also the one kicking the lawn mower, and pulling and pushing on locked doors, wildly enough to loosen the foundations of a house. It is possible this man had children in order to operate machinery for him. Yes, I think so.

My dad is a sportswriter. He also writes children's fiction under a pseudonym. In these books, he writes about small children organizing the world around them despite themselves, a world full of human failures, cranks and despots, some with endearing and poignant flaws, others with thunderous bad taste and hilariously inflated egos. He finds these types, these faltering embarrassing types, really funny. These are his people.

To relax, my sportswriting dad watches sports on TV. He would like to be watching TV right now and he hears my little sister's dancing step close by.

"Harriet!"

My sister dances in. She is five years old and taking ballet classes. She has the right build but lacks discipline. She is a little too exuberant and has no time for the formality of steps.

"Yeee-ess?"

"Will you pass the remote."

"Oh Daddy, no! There are bad gamma rays, Jem told me. And soon you will fall asleep, snore-snore-noisy! Just like at the zoo, Ben said. No, Daddy, no, no! Hello! Goodbye!"

My sister is merry and exits with pirouettes and fouettés.

"Goddamnit!"

Ben races past, a flurry of long limbs. He is usually in a hurry and my dad is not quick enough to catch him. Nor does he always know what to say, how to get his attention. Ben is complicated. I am crazy about him and this is not a problem for me. You have to know how to get through, that's all.

"Hey, Jude," my dad calls from his prone sofa position.

Jude, who was only passing, backtracks and stands in the doorway of the living room. My brother Jude is a man of few words. He doesn't see much point in talking a lot. He has a bagel in one hand and a book in the other.

"Pass me the remote. Did you mow the lawn yet?"

"Not yet," Jude says, unruffled, moving very slowly in the vague direction of the remote control. He picks up a magazine on the way and bites his bagel. He is easily distracted and never in a hurry.

"JUDE!"

I am looking for Jude. There he is.

"Ahh! Jem! Who's my favorite child?"

"What do you want, Dad?"

I wish I had not come in, but I want Jude. Being bossed around and doing silly tasks for your dad when wearing a holster and cowboy hat is seriously disrupting.

"Stick 'em up!" he says, laughing.

I would quite like to shoot him now but I can't. Never shoot an unarmed man.

This is how it was when we were small kids. It is still a bit like this when we come home to visit, even today. We all have our own machines now and we know how to use them. We don't ask anyone else. We laugh now mostly about my dad when he is thumping machinery with the full expectation that this will be effective. We smile and try to help out. I think he likes that. Once, though, I saw him try to light a faulty boiler with a match. I wanted to yell at him but could not. I took over the situation but I could not yell at him. He is not a kid, he is my dad.

5. ALWAYS GO TO THE LOO IF YOU THINK YOU MAY NEED TO PEE.

Here are the times when passing up on rule number five is a bad idea. (1) Settling into a cinema or theater seat and the show is about to begin. Too late. (2) Sitting at your table in a posh restaurant and ordering wine and food. The entrée arrives. Too late. (3) Turning off the lights at night when in bed in fetal position and already half-asleep. Too late. Now you will have tortured dreams featuring gruesome toilet-bowl situations. (4) Car rides with grumpy drivers.

I want to blame my dad for this but that is not the way things work just now. In the world today, all things dark and tumultuous are down to me. My dad's mood is definitely my fault and I cannot bear to hold up the terrible car journey, the fifteen-minute ride which my dad conveys to me with a look will be as grueling as a forced march across all the central provinces of Canada. No, I cannot hold up the journey by asking to dash to the loo first. My dad says we are going NOW. Some people rub their hands in glee and say, Now! Others, like my dad, mean only one thing by "now." Now is full of terror.

O-KAAAY . . . co-RAAAALL! O-KAAAAY . . . co-RAAALLL! I think of this, too, that my dad must believe if he thumps me, if he takes me by the shoulders and rattles my little bones, gives me a shake momentous enough to reorganize all my vital organs and charge up my circulation and spark up all the neurons and synaptic impulses in my cerebellum, that I, too, will function again. It's a simple operation. Come back, Jem. Howdy, partner. Long time no see.

We're there now. Parking, my dad nearly mows down two dumpy ladies wearing stretchy trousers in appalling colors, but it doesn't even raise a chuckle in our wagon. In good times this would be a great game, using our car like a cowcatcher. Not today, though.

"Okay. I'm waiting here. Five minutes," he announces, not even looking at us, reaching behind the seat for a newspaper and snapping it open at the sports pages.

Mum and I see right away that the chemist/health shop is closed. Oh-oh. Clearly they knew I was coming.

"Let's get ice cream," my mother says recklessly, not glancing back at the car.

This feels pretty dangerous. I am prickly all over.

I get a tub of coffee ice cream and my mother, almost uniquely refined in her tastes and a really great cook, opts for something truly disgusting with caramel and scary little bits all over the top. For her, this is a throwback to a happy childhood she never actually had. She looks rebellious and gleeful which is cool to behold.

Walking back to the car, I note two things. I don't need to pee anymore. And my dad is storming toward us, his hands flapping angrily like someone has stolen the car from right under him or maybe a war has begun and we are behind enemy lines. Spotting the tubs of ice cream takes him to a point beyond fury, a place Mum and I do not want to be. I look at her. I am scared now but she smiles beautifully and makes for the car, getting in the back with me. My dad returns to the driver's seat and tugs the door closed, but he can't slam it because his car is posh and new and he has to be a bit careful.

"Aren't you sitting in front?" he asks crossly.

"No," she says, and then, more quietly, "Home, James."

I feel a great whirl of hilarity in my stomach now and I look at my mother with shock and delight. I whisper, "Home, James" too. I keep saying it in my head and glancing at her. We eat our ice creams all the way home. I did not get my remedy for depression, but then of course, maybe I did, for a minute or two at least, which is perhaps all a person should rightly expect, I don't know.

6. HAVE A CATALOGUE OF JOKES OR JOKEY SITUATIONS YOU CAN HAUL UP FROM MEMORY IN DARK TIMES.

You have to work pretty hard at rule number six. Sometimes, not very grown-up jokes are the best. For instance, my brother Gus and I often look at each other across a room and thrust out our lower mandibles, curling the mouth up at the corners, adopting a crazed, wide-eyed expression. Pretty soon we are spluttering into our drinks. It only takes a second. It is not grown-up but it is very reliable for a laugh, whereas jokes about German philosophers are not.

My dad tells one or two jokes I have never understood. One of them involves fishing and gefilte fish. It goes something like this.

What happened to all the herring fished out of the X sea? Well! Ha ha ha! It ends up as gefilte fish in Chicago! My dad chokes up and all the sophisticates around him quake with mirth, shoulders akimbo and so on. The second joke is about an Eskimo. My dad went up to the Arctic once to cover some sledging championships or something for *Sports Illustrated* and he came back with some bizarre souvenirs, such as a sealskin doll for Harriet which smelled so bad she wouldn't touch it and I buried it in the garden for her, plus some pretty bad jokes. It seems that when Eskimos had to choose English names for themselves for legal reasons or something, they picked whatever favorite activity they had or whatever object they were close to at the time. One lady was a fan of American football and so she called herself Sophie Football. Absolutely hilarious.

Here is another joke my dad finds very funny indeed. One afternoon in late August when I was fourteen or so, I cross the kitchen of our summer cottage on my way outside and see my dad finishing a snack involving bread and tomatoes and spring onions.

"Hey, Jem."

I stop. Oh-oh. "Yup?" Will this take long? What does he want? I am aiming to go swimming.

"Come here." He crooks his finger at me. This drives me wild. Having to get closer and closer just to be sent far off to get something for him.

"I'm here." I take one step closer, that's it.

"How much pocket money do I owe you?"

"June-July-August."

"I'll flip you double or nothing."

"I don't know."

"Come on, Jem." Be a man.

"Okay then."

I lose. My dad is so happy, he is just delirious with mirth. He goes looking for some more of his kids right away. He tries it out on Harriet and Gus and wins both times. This is one of the funniest things that has happened in the whole of my dad's life, it seems. He tells the story for years and years. This is the kind of thing that keeps him going.

It is possible, when my dad is stuck in a queue at the supermarket or in a traffic jam, he calls up these jokes, and things improve for him right then, he feels better. You have to find your own thing. My mother saying "Home, James" in a very quiet blithe voice the day we came back from our abortive trip to the chemist that summer, on a quest for some stupid herbal remedy for depression, that makes me smile, it really does, anytime I think of it.

Here is a joke. Can you be a cowboy if you are Jewish? I do not know the punchline. One day I'll ask my dad, who is Jewish and a cowboy, maybe the only one that ever lived.

7. ALWAYS CARRY A BOOK WITH YOU.

This is a very important rule and easy to slip up on. Here is how. You say to yourself, I have carried that book with me every single day this week and never once have I had time to pull it out and read it. It is making a big fat unseemly bulge in my pocket, it is bumping up against my hip when I walk, it is weighing me down. Today I am not taking it, goddamnit. That is the day your friend is forty minutes late and you are left at the restaurant with the foot of your crossed leg swinging loose and you have studied every face and every painting in the place. That is the day your bus gets caught in a traffic jam or you end up having to take someone to the emergency room and wait four hours for the person to emerge. Always carry a book with you.

Here, though, are two times I had a book with me and it was of no use.

This was the first time. It is my turn for the emergency room. I am there because I cut my hand pretty badly and sometime between diving onto the floor of my flat in a petrified faint and getting into a cab to the hospital, I grab a novel and slip it into my coat pocket. I have paid attention to rule number seven, yes I have. I choose *Le père Goriot* by Honoré de Balzac, which I am reading for the second time. But when I am in Casualty, I am too sick to read. I am too sick and too scared. The nurse tries to speed me through. He asks, "Why are you so cold? How did this happen?"

I don't know, I answer. I don't feel well. I was cutting a bagel. I say this about the bagel because I have just read in a leaflet from a bagel shop that bagel-cutting injuries are a really common occurrence. I remember the bagel legend, too. How a Jewish baker invented the bagel in 1683 to commemorate the good deed performed by King Jan III of Poland. His good deed was this: he saved Vienna from a Turkish invasion. The bread was in the shape of a stirrup due to Jan's love of equestrianism. In Austria the word for stirrup is *Buegel*. The name of the shop where I found the leaflet is Angel Bagel. Where was my angel tonight? Drunk somewhere, high on single malt. Nowhere for me. The thing is, I am lying about the bagel-cutting injury.

"What are all those other cuts?" the nurse asks.

"I was reaching into a cupboard and I grazed my wrist on a cheese grater, how stupid can you get?" I say in a rush.

If my dad saw me now with my cut-up wrists, he would be really

really mad at me, although he would not say a thing. He would unstrap my holster and take away my gun. He would unpin my tin star. You are not fit to ride with me, that is what he would mean to tell me. You are no longer my right-hand man.

This brings me to rule number eight.

8. WHEN YOU ARE GOING THROUGH DARK TIMES, PACK UP YOUR KNIVES AND GIVE THEM TO A FRIEND.

I mean all of them, all your knives. If you are at all inclined to slice yourself up in dark times, to pretend you are a tomato, which is an ideal fruit for testing the sharpness of filleting knives, carpet cutters, cleavers, X-acto blades, Stanley knives and safety razor blades, to watch with fascination as the blood rises to the surface in particularly sensitive zones of your body such as wrists and ankles, then rule number eight is one for you. It will mean an expensive period of shopping at Marks & Spencer for ready meals, ones with bite-sized pieces of prawn or chicken in chili tomato sauce, for instance. Or you can buy pricey pots of tomato sauce or roasted aubergines to put on pasta. Italian clam sauces are available in small jars from the best Italian delis. Or you can just eat a lot of yogurt and nuts and mashed banana. Buy bread in small shapes, i.e., bagels, or *baguette de tradition* you can break off bits from. It will be all right. If you feel like eating during dark times, you will not go hungry in a house empty of knives.

The second time I paid attention to rule number seven (ALWAYS CARRY A BOOK WITH YOU) and it was of no use to me was when my dad said goodbye to me before I took a coach to the airport on my way back home after my summer holiday, the one which featured the car ride and the quest for an herbal remedy for depression.

I have already waved to my mother. I asked her not to come with me because parting between us is a wrenching business, even for five minutes or so, even if we separate on a shopping expedition or something. I know I cannot go through the airport thing with her, no.

My dad lays his big hands on my little shoulders at the coach station, my two small cases at my feet. I am pretty sure my mother will have slipped some treat into my carry-on bag and I am looking forward to finding it as soon as my dad goes. Something about his two big hands on my shoulders just now has me worried. It feels ominous, like just before Joey warns Shane in the final shootout about the man aiming at him from the balcony. You know Shane cannot die, but he could. He could. He comes so close.

"Jem," says my dad in a lower voice than usual.

I glance at his face and then stare at his chest. "We have done everything we can. We love you. We don't know what else to do anymore. You have to look after yourself now. Got your ticket, passport, enough cash?"

"Yuh."

"We'll see you in a few months. We love you."

As I watch him walk away from me, a slightly lurching walk, heels making their mark on the ground, arms swinging a little and the hands hovering loose but ready at holster height, I think, One shot. One shot is all it would take.

No, Jem, no. Never shoot a man in the back. Don't you remember anything?

I want to scream after him, too. I want to scream, "Do you love me right now, though? Do you even like me now? Do you?" But I just get on the coach and stare out of the window into the evening through a veil of tears, and at the airport I cannot read or eat the nice treats my mother stashed for me, I am good for nothing. My dad does not love me and I am on my own, I have to look out for myself, okay. These are my first steps in that direction and all I can do is pace up and down the airport lounge and cry quietly. There are no prizes for behavior like mine and even rule number seven is of no use to me, goddamnit. I am thinking of making a pyre of my rule book or ripping it up in tight angry irretrievable pieces to flutter over the ocean. Tomorrow maybe. And I will never watch a western again. I hate westerns now.

9. ALWAYS HAVE SOME SPORTS NEWS AT HAND FOR WHEN YOUR DAD IS IN HOSPITAL AFTER A SCARY OPERATION TO DO WITH A FATAL DISEASE.

I've got my sports news ready in case my dad can talk to me, even for a few seconds. There was a tumor in him, they cut it out. My dad could have done this himself. Take a shot of cognac, stuff a hanky in your mouth, polish the knife on a rock, cut it out. Like snakebite, no problem. Today I might get to speak to him. Everyone is there with my mother—Ben, Jude, Harriet and Gus, even Ben's wife and Gus's girlfriend, who is pregnant. They have all flocked to him from wherever they live and are running and fetching and worrying and trying to joke with Mum and making calls to the outside world. I am the only one not there. Does he know it? Does he know I am not there? I am in the outside world. I just can't go. I cannot be there. I am on the outside, waiting for calls. Sometimes the boys explain things to me about the operation, but I do not take it in. I have the same feeling when someone is explaining an abstruse political news item to me. It is a nightmare of information. I listen and nod and hope the person will shut up soon. I do not take it in. I tell myself, I'll work it out later, I'll find out for myself what this all means.

I have not washed properly in five days, I only splash at the sink. I eat bread and cheese and stay up watching videos of westerns, way into the night, when it is only afternoon for my dad and the family. I watch *The Gunfighter*, *Gunfight at the O.K. Corral*, *My Darling Clementine*, and *Shane*. *Shane* is my favorite of all time.

"He'd never have been able to shoot you if you'd seen him!"

"Bye, little Joe."

"He'd never even have cleared the holster, would he, Shane?"

"Shane? Shane! Come back! . . . Bye, Shane!"

Finally, Mum puts my dad on the phone.

"Hey, Dad."

"You are going to be fine," he says.

What?

"YOU-are-going-to-be-JUST-FINE."

"You mean *you* are going to be just fine, right? You. How are you, Dad?"

"Everything is going to be all right, you are going to be fine, we are going to be—"

He *does* mean me.

"Dad?"

"Jem, you are—"

"Dad? Are you okay?"

"I am okay! I am o-KKKAAY—"

I clasp the receiver even tighter and jump up from a sitting position. I join in. "O-KKAAAY . . . co-RRAAAL, o—" but my mother has taken the phone from him and I don't know now. I do not know if he was really singing the tune from *Gunfight at the O.K. Corral* or not.

Mum stays on the line for only a second or two, enough time to say she'll call back later or tomorrow and I hang up and sit in the dark room and feel cut off and panicky and manacled by this question. I want to know if my dad was doing the tune from the western with Burt Lancaster and Kirk Douglas playing Wyatt Earp and Doc Holliday. I need to know. And I wonder if the whisky-soaked angels are still hanging out with my dad, if they are hovering over the hospital, getting all confused, some of them keeling over suddenly and looking surprised and silly. What is going on here? That must be morphine! Some of them want to go, but the big-cheese angel says, Hang in there, this man is a gunfighter and he will get up to pour single malt another day. That's right, guys, I think. Hang in there.

That is rule number ten. HANG IN THERE.

I practice it, the gunslinger squint.

Hang in there.

PARTY SPIRIT

I am eight years old and I am home from school. I'm at my first convent, the one where the nuns are Irish. Harriet comes with me now, she is five. I have to look out for her because she is a little wild and gets scuffy knees and her fair hair flies about in an unruly fashion. It's like angel hair. Despite her likeness to an angel, the nuns prefer her to be neat and not run around like a wild thing. They like neat angels at my convent. So I look out for Harriet at my school, I keep my eye on her, in the playground, in the echoing corridors and hallways and in the high-ceilinged dining room, places where there are dangers for Harriet, things such as stones and puddles, sharp bits of molding and hard tiled floors. I saw her fly right into a French window once, as if she could dance right through it into the courtyard. Harriet feels that if you can see through glass, you can skip right through it to the other side, why not. I have quite a lot of tolerance for this behavior in my sister because I know how she thinks. She is high-spirited. The nuns say this, "Your sister is high-spirited," meaning can't you stop her from running all over the place, especially out of bounds. The grounds at my convent are pretty extensive and you can easily stray into out-of-bounds areas, especially if you are Harriet and pay no attention to instructions regarding out-of-bounds areas. Never mind. We are home now, we got here safely and she is out of my hands for a while. Harriet dashes off to find Mum, who is probably with Gus. She drops things on the way, hat, gloves, satchel. Even in summer we wear gloves at school, white ones. Harriet does not like a lot of extra haberdashery. Angels are not keen on heavy clothes, I guess.

I need a snack. Oh great, binoculars. Mum has been to Zetland's. This is a bakery and they make fantastic rolls that resemble pairs of binoculars. When Jude and I are World War II British commandos, we use them as binoculars until we get tired and need a snack, whereupon we eat them.

I take half a binocular. Ben is standing near the kitchen table, his feet crossed, one of them bent at the ankle and splayed out to the side. I like the way he tangles up. He has one hand in the nut and raisin bowl which Mum always puts out for him as he is crazy for nuts and raisins and likes something you can eat steadily but is already in small pieces.

He is looking at me expectantly.

"Hey," I say. "Hey, Ben."

"Hey," he answers, with staring eyes.

Ben is not ready to tell me what he wants to tell me. Okay. I am patient. I decide on the other binocular half and sit down at the long white oak table, on the chair I learned to make bows on, so I could tie my own shoes. We all did this. We sat on the floor while Mum cooked and she'd tie a shoelace on the strut of a chair back and we'd tie and untie until we got it right. She'd feed us little slivers of vegetable or something while we practiced.

Eating my binocular and waiting for Ben to come out with it, I think about finishing up my homework in time to watch *The Wizard of Oz* with everyone tonight. This film is free, in other words, we do not have to pull out time from the bank to watch it. We are only allowed one hour of television a day and have to save up for things, except free things such as *The Wizard of Oz* or *To Kill a Mockingbird* or *The Grapes of Wrath*. *The Grapes of Wrath* is an old film and pretty depressing. I didn't really want to watch the whole thing. It featured scrawny types at campsites surrounded by horrible dilapidated vehicles spilling rickety belongings and little kids in flimsy clothing. They huddled around fires and ate sloppy food out of tin saucers and kept driving to different sites, working all day and getting more and more depressed and saying brave things in short gloomy sentences. I had to stay and watch though, because Dad was sitting up on the sofa, instead of lying down, meaning, this is an important viewing experience, Jem. You stay.

Other free programs are documentaries about Nazis. Now I cannot look at anyone wearing up and down stripy pyjamas. Clearly they have not watched as many documentaries about Nazis as I have.

Here is one thing my dad always asks me whenever we watch documentaries about Nazis.

"Jem?"

I break out of my reverie, which has to do with wanting to play Action Man with Jude right now and not watching a gruesome documentary featuring death.

"Yes?"

"You're not making the sign of the cross or anything like that at school, are you?"

He gives me a stern look, his dark brown irises fixing me from the corners of his eyelids, the skin bunching up there for emphasis. How can I say yes to a look like that, daring me to say yes but expecting no? My dad has brown eyes and all the rest of us are various shades of blue. At school, they said in biology that women carry the dominant genes for eye color. Mum has blue eyes. My dad is Jewish. My mum is Protestant. I am wondering who carries the dominant genes for religion.

"No, Dad,"

I do, though.

Sometimes, when no one is looking, I make the sign of the cross. In the name of the Father and the Son and the Holy Ghost, ah-men. Then we learned to say Holy Spirit, not Ghost, due to modernism. I liked Ghost better. Never mind. I watch the girls do this at assembly and I never join in. I am Jewish, can't they see that? It's cool, being different. On my own though, sometimes I try it out, this cross in the air, touching forehead and shoulders and heart, just to see, and it feels spooky, like lying or stealing, neither of which I am good at, betraying myself with blushes and a racing heart and a stark look in my eyes. My mum is a Protestant but I am pretty sure she does not do any of that stuff, signs of the cross and genuflection and so on. I don't think she needs to because she may not come from Earth like we do, she may come from elsewhere, where they do things their own way. I've been watching her closely and I am on the case. I am gathering clues all the time.

"Ben?" Come on, Ben.

"Yeh?"

"Do you think they'll let me stay up to see the whole thing? Do you?"

"Oh yes," says Ben. "It's a classic. You know."

Oh. I am beginning to worry there may be Nazis in this film because besides being a free film, I will not, it seems, have to go to bed in the middle of it. This is the other impediment to sheer viewing pleasure in our house. Bedtime. I have huddled on the sofa with Jude, watching some war film not classic enough, such as *The Great Escape*, not even able to concentrate, knowing bedtime was a few paces away, listening out for the gentle swish of my mother and those two words from the doorway, "Jem. Bedtime."

Once, when my dad was watching with us, I tried to argue, to fight for my rights. Most kids I knew stayed up all hours and there was no TV rationing. They did not have to smuggle sweets into their homes, either, no, and they could even read Enid Blyton books, forbidden in our house due to prejudiced views expressed in dodgy writing.

"Please can I stay up?"

" 'May I,' do you mean? Anyone *can* stay up," my mother says gently.

"Yes. May I? Please."

"Oh, darling. It will come round again." I hate this. Promises to do with days and times beyond contemplation. You'll feel better soon. It'll be over before you know it. We can buy another one. I'll be back. All these assurances without places and dates are no good to me.

"When though? What if I go blind? What if I do not have a TV later in life and the film has come round again?"

"Jem," my dad says, sensing hysteria.

"What if I just don't notice it is on? What if I don't even want to watch it then? What if I'm too busy or I have a TV and it is broken? What if—"

"JEM!"

Then my mother speaks. She is standing in the doorway, she is leaning into the frame, her head tilted to one side, her hands clasped loosely in front. "Jem. Bedtime." And suddenly all the noise goes out of the world and bed seems like the best place to go and I don't get this movie anyway. Where does all the fresh dark earth go when they are digging out the tunnels, where does all that wood come from, and the material for the uniforms? The guy going blind and the one with claustrophobia are a bit depressing and I am tired and I am going to bed. Jude, who is lying on his side, getting his usual sideways view of the TV, will explain it all to me tomorrow. He will tell me the good bits I missed, if he is in the mood. Mum holds out a hand for me, but I can't take it right away due to a cross feeling within. I am cross with my dad who is pretending to shoot a machine gun.

"Quick! Run for it! I'll cover you!" He is creased up with mirth but I ignore him, I do my best. Bloody.

I take Mum's hand at the foot of the stairs and it's the best grip in the world. It's loose, not too loose, firm not tight. She has long fingers and incredibly silky skin and the temperature is just right, cool not cold, and the feel is dry not rough, never rough. I take in all these details about her hand and the way she holds mine because I am not crazy for holding hands; I get squirmy and bad-tempered, I feel my fingers getting squashed or my elbow twisted and wrenched in the grip of most people. But I could hold my mum's hand and never let go, and stay happy, I know it. I may not believe in angels, I find the whole subject confusing. At the convent, for instance, I remember when my friend Christina's little brother died, having fallen out of a window playing hide and seek, the mother superior said at assembly, "Now let us all pray for Julian who is with the saints and angels in heaven." Then Christina cried, the first time I saw her do so, and I was mad at the nuns, all of them. No. No. He is not with the saints and angels in heaven.

Holding my mother's hand, I wonder if angels can sneak inside people, because I think this is what it must feel like to hold hands with one. It's a weird thought, but as I said, I have these suspicions about my mother.

"Jem," Ben says, ready to make an announcement.

I look at him, showing him I am ready too.

"I dreamed about Mummy and in the dream she was a witch and she looked like Cruella De Vil in *101 Dalmatians*. You know." His eyes have a spooked look.

"Whoa," I say.

"Yeah."

"Bloody!"

"Yeah."

I try to look spooked and nervous too, because I do not want to disappoint Ben. I know that a big part of having a gothic imagination like Ben's is making other people nervous about your gothic view of things, and I do not want to let my brother down, especially since it cost him so much to tell me this news. I even take in and let out a big breath and gaze at the floor and hold off finishing my binocular, which I'd really like to be eating. But I do not want to hear any more from Ben. Our mother does look like Cruella De Vil, if Cruella suddenly became a lovely character, and she even has that shock of white at her forehead, a zap of lightning almost, in a black sky. I like it. It's cool. So this Cruella business does not strike me as at all gothic, but the witch part is a bit worrying and if my mother does strange witch type things in this dream, I do not want the details, no thank you.

"Whoa. Bloody," I repeat. "Ben, I am going to do my homework so I can see the film with you, okay?"

"Sure," he says, still giving me a spooky look. "Okay."

I need to change out of my uniform and as I push open the door of the room I share with my sister, I get ready for Harriet to leap out at me from somewhere, from the cupboard or behind the door. This is something she really enjoys doing and I always act really scared so she can have a good time. Today Harriet does not fly at me. She must have grown bored waiting for me as I was so long downstairs with Ben.

I put on jeans and one of Jude's old rugby tops. I like to wear Jude's old clothes. I plan to do my homework outside at the wrought-iron table on the terrace with all the cherub statues standing all around. Statuary, Mum calls it. Some of the statues are not cherubs but naked grown-ups carrying sheaves of wheat and scythes and things or carrying nothing at all but looking wistful, leaning their weight on one leg. I like doing my homework there.

Here comes Ben. Now what?

"Can I come in?"

"*May* I."

"Yeh-yeh."

"Sure, what is it, Ben?"

"About that dream. I just want to say, it doesn't mean Mum is a witch, but I do happen to think she is descended from Druids."

"What do you mean, descended?" I am feeling restless now.

"They are her ancestors. Druids."

"Like in Astérix?"

"Yup."

"Okay, Ben. Going outside now. Aren't Druids all men?"

"Descended from, I said. She can still have the powers, though."

"Oh. Well, see you in a bit." I step lightly around him.

With my homework stuff is my Mummy casebook. In Sherlock Holmes there is always a casebook and I am making a case. I have a list of observations, only one per page, leaving space for special remarks and so on.

These words are written in a column on page one. *Spirit. Ghost. Angel. Witch. God. Fairy. Conjurer.* Conjurer is a good word I heard. I looked it up and wrote in the definition in case I forget exactly what it means. Not the conjurer bit, because I don't get that at all: "one who practices legerdemain." What is legerdemain? I don't have time to look this up. Conjure, though, is good: "produce magical effects by natural means, perform marvels." Okay.

After this come two words I saw in my dad's thesaurus, which is a book that gave me a bit of a headache. I had enough words already except for adding these two: *Enchanter. Diviner.* I do not think diviner is right so I have put in square brackets like this: [ ]. I like diviner, though, because it makes me think "more divine" and Mum says this word sometimes. "Divine!" Also, it is a word that comes from the Latin for God. Or a god. And here is a definition of divine: "superhumanly excellent, gifted or beautiful." That sounds like her, it just does.

Next comes a list of clues.

1. Mummy's touch feels different from anyone else's.

2. Mummy is very beautiful, not at all like any other mums I have seen or even non-mums.

3. Mummy's voice feels good to hear, not tickling the ears or giving you a headache like almost everyone else's. It feels like the moment just before you fall asleep, or before you take a bite of binocular. Even though very soft, it is easy to pick out in a room full of people or very far away, like it is supersonic.

4. She drinks potions.

This is true. Somedays, I come home from school and she is mixing up a potion in a blender. It is usually green or orange or very white. I have never seen anyone do this before. I do not want to act as if I am on the case, so I slide up onto a chair and I ask her about it, very casual.

"Mum? What's that?"

"Lunch!"

It is pretty late for lunch. It is four o'clock. I don't say this though. I say, "It looks funny."

"It is full of goodness," she says, smiling that smile.

"Can I, may I taste it?"

"I don't think you'll like it, Jem. How about a binocular?"

You see, Jem?

I write in clue number five.

5. Ben says Mummy = maybe a witch or a Druid. Descended from a Druid with Druid powers.

I add this word *Druid* to the column on page one.

Here comes Jude with some heavy books. I wish I were at a

boys' school because the books look a lot better to me than ours, which are a bit sissy, with a lot of illustrations. I wish I were at Jude's school so we could be together all the time. He would watch out for me. But who would watch over Harriet? It's a problem.

Jude pauses halfway toward me to think about something and stare out at the garden for a bit, then he sits at the wrought-iron table.

"Mum brought binoculars," he tells me.

"I know. I already had one. What homework have you got?" I ask.

"History. Latin. Chemistry."

"I've got sums."

"Maths."

"Maths." They even have tougher names for things at boys' schools. "Jude?"

He spreads out his books but he does not open them. He just takes them in, the weight of it all.

"Ben dreamt Mummy was a witch."

Jude frowns a little and shuffles his books around. I notice because he does not frown a lot usually. He is pretty serious all the time but does not need to frown, which takes energy and he is very decisive about spending energy, choosing carefully. He almost never runs, for instance, unless it is strictly necessary.

"She always knows what I'm thinking," he says quite slowly, gazing at his books.

"Bloody," I say, knowing him never to exaggerate.

"Here. I got you this," adds Jude, handing over four pieces of Black Cat bubble gum, my favorite gum. "And don't have it now. It's too close to supper. She'll know."

"Okay. Thanks, Jude." This gum is probably stolen goods.

Never mind. Jude never steals just for himself. He always has treats for me, and usually Ben. Not Harriet, though. She'd blab by mistake.

I write down in my casebook:

6. She always knows what Jude is thinking. What I'm thinking, too.

I write this due to suddenly remembering a particular day when I decided, I don't know why, not to speak until suppertime. It was a Saturday and I was home all day, out in the garden, inside, in and out, around. Anytime I came into the house for a snack, or a glass of water, or just to say hi and find out what was up, if there were some good game going, Ben or Jude doing something interesting, if I came across Mum, she'd glance at me and smile that smile. Bloody. I think she's on to me. I turn on the tap for some water I don't really want, just to check it out, see if she knows.

"Well, I guess we won't be hearing from Jem until supper," she says, a bit sly, raising one eyebrow and looking out of the kitchen window.

Sometimes she gives me letters to post on the way to school. I always forget and come back home with them but I stuff the envelopes into the lining of my coat where there is a rip so she won't know, just in case she is on the hunt for sweet wrappers and wants to feel in our pockets. All I have to do is say I forgot, but I don't, because I feel silly that I forgot this one little thing she asked me to do. I complicate things, I see signs of this all the time.

"Don't forget to post my letters tomorrow, Jem," she says on her way out of my room, after tucking me in that night.

Don't forget to post my letters tomorrow. It's definitely weird.

And that's not all. I am noting new things all the time.

Sister Catherine is the first-year teacher. She teaches the four-year-old kids and when you are a four-year-old kid, the older kids chant this at you as you cross the long, echoing corridor on the way to the dining room, carrying your small wooden chair, fit for a four-year-old kid. "Babies, babies, babies." Like this is something really pathetic to be. I don't chant this myself at the four-year-olds, being above this kind of thing and especially when Harriet was in Sister Catherine's class. Sister Catherine walks up and down the paneled dining room, in the space between the rows of wooden refectory tables, wearing her cutoff Ebenezer Scrooge gloves and muttering to herself. The babies sit at a special table of their own at the far end. It's low so they can fit their little forearms on it, although not their elbows. "Elbows *off* the table," says Sister Catherine. Pacing up and down, she reminds me of the Roman sea captain in *Ben Hur* who keeps upping the rowing speed until the slaves start fainting, keeling over in their manacles and getting whipped by sweaty types in loincloths and leather bracelets.

Sometimes Sister Catherine will pick on a kid and decide she needs help eating. Let's say the kid has a look of dismay on her face, meaning, What is this on my plate and why do I have to eat it? The nun always says, Think of the starving children in India, and the kid has an urge to say, Please wrap this up and send it to them right now. Thank you. There are even "sacrifice days" wherein pudding is placed in front of you and all of a sudden Sister Catherine says,

"This is sacrifice day."

Now you have to give your pudding back. This is only ever a day when it is something you can actually eat without having a throw-uppy feeling, i.e. a piece of cake not swimming in rhubarb juice and custard, or one of those strange cylinders of ice cream wrapped in cardboard exactly like a roll of toilet paper. Sacrifice days never fall on rice pudding or semolina day, times I have taken to feeling suddenly struck down by illness and am sent off to see Sister Martha, my favorite nun who is also the nurse.

Sister Martha is younger than the other nuns and she is very pretty. She knows what's up. She goes through the motions, though, patting my forehead and taking my temperature. I rate her touch quite highly. It's not at all unpleasant. She only sends me back when the rice pudding has been safely cleared away and she has asked me a few questions about football. She is a football fan and fond of Bobby Charlton. I gave her a picture of him once that came out of a pack of chocolate cigarettes Jude stole for me.

The kid with the look of dismay on her face is usually me and so Sister Catherine decides to help me eat. This is how she does it. She comes up behind my back and presses her squat shape into me, her arms reaching over my shoulders, bending my neck so my head is nearly in the plate, nearly causing me irreparable damage to the spinal column. She picks up my knife and fork and begins her work, involving ferocious mashing of peas and cutting up of Spam and mixing it all together.

"There," she says, satisfied, raising herself back up.

"Thank you, Sister," I chant, meanwhile gazing with fear at my plate. Then I think two things. One. I pray, yes I pray, she never does this to Harriet because Harriet cannot abide her various foodstuffs touching each other on the plate. *Not touching!* she will wail. I hope I am around if it ever happens. Harriet will need me. Two. I dream of home. I dream of Mum and her way with food, how everything looks beautiful and tastes magical, how watching her prepare meals, sneaking looks while I am supposed to be doing my homework at the oak table where I like to work just to be near her, sneaking looks I know she is aware of, every little action of hers, a slice, a chop, a stir, has the power to mesmerize.

"If you finish your work," she says without even turning to see me sneaking a look, "you can help me." There she goes again.

Staring at my Spam and peas, I dream of supper and I wish for shepherd's pie, shepherd's pie in little individual casseroles for Ben, Jude, Harriet and me and a big one for Mum and Dad. When I get home, I walk straight into the kitchen from the back door, noticing that I can clear the big stone step much more easily now. Harriet needs a bit of a leg up still. Then I smell it.

Shepherd's pie, Jem. In little casseroles and one big casserole. Mum turns around, smiling that smile, looking at her girls, Harriet and me.

"We haven't had shepherd's pie in a long time, have we, girls?" Mum says, ready to catch a flying Harriet. I am speechless.

As I said, it's definitely weird.

I am lying in bed thinking about *The Wizard of Oz*, which was pretty good although I think there were Nazis in it. The guards at the Wicked Witch of the West's castle looked a lot like Nazis to me, the way they were marching all around the ramparts, kicking their toes straight into the air without bending their knees. When the wicked witch dies—"I'm mel-ting, I'm mel-ting"—they convert into very charming characters. I found this conversion a little spooky. Worst of all were the flying monkeys with bellhop hats. I am glad Harriet missed out on that bit, in fact she did not last very long at all, bursting into tears when the Lollipop Guild came on. My dad loves that part. Mum took her up to bed. After the film, we sat around for a few minutes and Dad kept singing the Lollipop Guild song and shaking with mirth, and Mum said when she first saw *The Wizard of Oz* she didn't want to be Dorothy but Glinda, the Good Witch of the North, played by Billie Burke.

Very interesting. I made a note of this.

Dad also told us for the eighteenth time that when he went to the movies as a kid, a double feature cost about two pence and you had money left over for sweets, etc, etc. Ben, Jude and I give him blank looks, so maybe he'll give up on the double feature plus ice cream story one day soon. And maybe not.

Suddenly I hear sniffles. I see a small person in the middle of my bedroom with a halo of fluffy blond hair, glowing a little in the dark. It's Harriet.

"Harriet?"

"Mummy's a witch. Ben said." She's all out crying now.

"He told you?"

"Heard him."

Oh-oh. "Were you in here, Harriet?"

"Hiding. Waiting for you. Under the bed."

I gather up Harriet and we climb onto the windowsill. We have a big bay window in our room and if Harriet has a bad dream we usually sit up there and play cards, even though she never remembers the rules to a single game, or we play with shadows, making little beasties with our hands. And she likes me to sing to her, she is the only person who does. At the convent, I have to sing separately from everyone else due to my voice being too deep, and I stand on a single chair with all the other girls squashed up on benches, singing all together in a regular fashion. It's quite a horrible experience and I want to tell the nun who teaches singing, if you can't sing high you probably can't sing low either so why don't we just skip it? I sing okay for Harriet, though, maybe because she likes it so much.

"Shall I do a song, Harriet?"

"No. Explain."

Oh no. "Okay. Remember in the film, the bad witch?"

"The bicycle lady."

"That's right. That's a bad witch. Then the lady who comes in the soap bubble when everything was all in color?"

"Brenda."

"No. Glinda. Glinda, the Good Witch of the North."

"Glinda is not a name."

"It's her name, Harriet. It's a good witch type name, okay?"

"Okay."

"That's like Mummy. That's what Ben meant, okay?"

"Now sing."

I sing for Harriet.

Next morning, Harriet is eating a binocular by taking the smallest bites I have ever seen a human take and she keeps staring at Mum, who is helping everyone with breakfast and playing with Gus all at the same time. I hope I look like her when I grow up, I really do. Harriet's behavior is making me anxious. "Glinda," she says. "Glinda-Glinda-Glinda."

I grab my sister. "Come on, Harriet. We'll be late. You can eat that on the way."

It's really embarrassing. I also can't help feeling that Mum knows exactly what this is all about. Jude was right. On the way to school, I think about what he said and about clue number six, but I see that it is not just that she knows what you are thinking but what has happened, and even what might happen, like she's right there with you, but invisible.

7. She can see without looking. Sometimes Mum takes these little naps. "Ten minutes!" she says, in a really cheery way. I have

timed her, sitting cross-legged outside her door or around the corner, and it's always ten minutes exactly and with her eyes still closed, around the nine minute and fifty-eight second mark, she says, "Hello, Jem."

When I get close to her, she opens her eyes and smiles and looks like she's never even been asleep, not like me, for instance, always grumpy and messy when I wake up. And she knew I was there. She knew it was me.

I am in trouble over transubstantiation. I will not forget this word in a hurry, ever since Mum explained the whole business to me. Hearing about it in catechism, a class I am not supposed to be part of, aroused feelings of distress in me. I could not understand how this ritual—Here is my body, here is my blood—could make anyone feel better about things. I also thought this must have been very confusing to natives in countries where all those missionaries were very busy turning cannibals into Catholics. It's all very odd but Mum cleared it up for me, adding a caution or two. She said there is an important difference between the Catholic and Protestant view of things and that I should not really discuss it at the convent. Then she suggested I not bring it up with Dad, not unless she is around. Okay.

I sorted Harriet out, too, on the subject of transubstantiation, although I left the actual word out in case she tries it out on Dad, who will then get all worried about signs of the cross, etc., etc. Harriet was pretty freaked out about the flesh and the blood and what some of her friends do on Sundays, according to the nuns.

"Disgusting. Disgusting disgusting!" she cried.

"Harriet. Stop it. It's not really blood or flesh, okay, it's just a symbol. It's like it, but not it, okay?"

"Yuck."

"Harriet. You are not supposed to be in catechism class."

"Catechism." Harriet looks worried. She has forgotten this word.

"When they talk about things like that. You read your book. You don't pay attention."

"I know. Read my book. Don't pay attention."

"Okay then." I try to be a bit stern, to close the subject.

Next day, when the little kids are all on a rest break, heads lying on their little forearms and Sister Catherine is telling that Last Supper story for the eighty-second time, Harriet pops her fluffy head up and says, "Not flesh and blood! It's pretend flesh and blood! Jem said!"

This is how I get into trouble over transubstantiation. I need to talk to Mum about it and it's nearly bedtime. Here comes Dad. He stops me as I try to enter the living room in my pyjamas.

"Where are you going, Jem?"

"I have to ask Mum something."

"Can I help?"

Definitely not. "Can't I just say good night?"

"Look, Jem, Mummy's busy. She—um."

My dad crouches down and puts his hands on my shoulders, weighing me down so I feel wobbly at the knees for a second. "Mummy's friend has, um, died and Mummy's very sad just now. You say good night and that's all, okay. Be very quiet. Go on." He twirls me around and gives me a gentle shove into the room but I can't see her. Where is she?

The French windows are open, Mum is outside on the terrace with the cherry trees, she's out there among the statuary, the cherubs and the naked ladies and the guys carrying sheaves of wheat and scythes. She is looking up at the sky and I follow her gaze and I see the stars are shining hard and bright. The stone slabs are cold under my feet, which is not a bad feeling.

Is she talking to me? She is talking to someone, very quietly. Then I know. She is talking to her friends. She is looking skyward at the stars and she is talking to friends. I don't want to interrupt. It's cold out here. Is she cold?

"It's okay, Jemima. You can come," says my mother without even turning around to make sure it's me, which reminds me of clue number seven. And it's me all right. I'm here. She stretches out her right hand for me, stretching it out behind her, and I move toward it and my whole body is prickling, like when you are in a lift that goes too fast and your body walks out on the ground floor but most of you is still on the fifth, up above.

I have nothing to say. She is crying, I can tell, even though it is pretty dark and she is so quiet and still. I am just about stunned by this. What do I do? I want to find Mum because she'd know what to do, she could fix this. Not this time. I want to give her something. What, though?

"Mum? Mummy? I. I want. I came to say good night."

"Jemima."

"Harriet brushed her teeth. I can tuck us both in."

"Good night, darling," she says. "Good night."

I start to leave her. I want to stay. I could just sit on a bench or over in the grass near the pond until she goes in. I know all her friends are out here but she might need me, too. I don't know.

"It's my bedtime, isn't it?"

"Yes, Jem, bedtime."

Okay.

I think I may need another section in my casebook. I need to write down this thing I just saw, this thing that breaks up the picture a little bit, this thing I am not sure is right for spirits to do. What is the opposite of a clue? Maybe I will call this section Not A Clue. Yes. Okay. The first not a clue is (1) Crying. I just don't think spirits are supposed to do this, except when a spirit is a spook, like Marley's Ghost, rattling the chains he forged in life. In this case, a spirit can make all kinds of noise, not just crying but moans, wails, whines, screeches and so on. This is a different situation altogether and connected to Ben's world, where things are dark and there are a lot of unhappy spirits with plans to haunt and spread fear in a general way. But crying is not something my kind of spirit does. I'll put the Not A Clue section right at the back of the book. I don't think I'll need a lot of space for that section. I don't think so.

I picture Mum in the garden, looking up at the sky, talking in a whispery voice and I realize something else and I know it will be another clue, clue number eight. (8) She has a lot of spirit friends and talks to them. Not just outside, tonight, but in museums. Right away I saw them all, when I was trying to work out if good spirits cry, all the angel types in those old paintings she takes me to see. Even if we are in some whole different part of the museum, she will breeze on by these paintings before we leave, as if to check up on them, check that they are still there. Now I understand that she was just saying hello to the angel types.

I do not have a big thing for paintings, but I like these. I wrote down the names of the painters. Duccio, Filippo Lippi, Mantegna, Bellini. I have seen them often due to my mother.

I can't remember any spirit-weeping going on in these paintings, although there is one, by Bellini, where two puny angels are having a hard time hauling Jesus up. They take hold of one arm each and Jesus is a lot bigger than them plus he is dead weight and the little angel kids have droopy expressions but I think this is just down to exertion, and sometimes tears can come out of this, but it doesn't really count as tears.

Another one I really like is called the Wilton Diptych. It is not by Wilton, they don't know who it is by, but it belonged to Richard II and it is painted on both sides. On the back there is a beautiful white hart, a symbol of Richard II's. That white hart reminds me of something every time I see it but I cannot think what. Anyway, Mum explained the diptych to me one day, also how Richard used this diptych for saying his prayers, although this strikes me as a little vain, especially as he is right in the painting himself and all the elegant blue angel ladies have little white hart badges like they are the Richard II fan club. I love these angel ladies in their long blue dresses because one has folded arms and one has her arm over the shoulder of the next lady and they look a tiny bit bored and fed up, dressed to go to a party. They are waiting for the ceremony to be over so they can bash off and have some fun. They remind me of my mother when she is dressing to go out.

At the gallery, I watch her looking at the paintings and she has a dreamy expression, like she is not really with me at all, and I guess that's what you look like if you have a big thing for paintings. Now I know the other reason she gets that dreamy expression. She is missing her friends.

Pretty soon after the trouble with transubstantiation, I have a bad
day because of Sister Teresa, the only mean nun at the convent.
She burst into our classroom this morning on the lookout as usual
for a victim. She is always discovering crimes and then goes on a
culprit hunt. She depends on hearsay for her accusations, she
never actually witnesses the crimes of name calling, pinching,
missing hair clips or sweets, which is probably why she is a nun
and not a policewoman. I hope she is not going to do a pocket
search today. That is a really grim event and reminds me of World
War II prisoner-of-war camp films. Because I do not leap out of
my chair right away and salute her, chanting "Good morning, Sister" in time with everyone else, she barks at me.

"Weiss! You are a very rude girl, Weiss."

She always calls me by my surname, something no other nun
does and she says it in a very pointed way ever since I corrected her
once, explaining how the *W* is pronounced like a *V.*

"Are you German," she asked me at the time, in a very suspicious manner.

"No."

"No, Sister."

"No, Sister."

"Why do you say '*ja*,' then?"

I wanted to say, "I don't say *ja*, I say yuh, which is very different, but I could not be bothered. She can think I'm German if
she wants to. When she shouts *Weiss!* at me, though, she is the
one acting like a Nazi officer in one of my Dad's favorite documentaries. And she is wrong. I am not a very rude girl. I win the
courtesy badge just about every two months due to my courteous

behavior. This nun has delusions about my character, like the singing nun, who looks at me all puzzled and sets me apart from all the other girls as if I were going to poison them with my deep voice. Maybe Sister Teresa thinks being Jewish is poisonous, too. It's possible.

All this has put me in a pretty bad mood and I need to tell Mum about it as soon as I get home. I hardly speak to Harriet on the way and I feel bad about this because in a minute she looks like a little bird shivering in the rain on a tree branch. It's really pathetic.

"Harriet, it's okay. It's not you."

"I didn't do anything."

"I know that."

"Sing!" she says, in her brightest voice.

"Maybe later, okay?"

"In the windowsill!"

"Yuh." *Ja.*

When we get home, Dad's at the back door, like he's been waiting for us. He picks Harriet up while she's scrambling up the big stone step, trying to do it without me.

"Hey, Dad." I shuffle past them.

"Jem, just a minute, where are you going? I have to talk to you." Harriet is playing with Dad's hair, pulling it over his face and giggling.

"In a minute, Dad," I say, then I hurry through the kitchen and up the stairs. I've had a bad day and I need Mum.

"Jem!" my dad calls out.

I don't understand what I am seeing outside my parents' bedroom. I see two men dressed up like soldiers in a war film. They are like stretcher bearers on a battlefield and on the stretcher is my mother. What is going on here? Is this a play? I don't think so. The men are taking her away.

I have a memory flash. I am sitting in our window with Harriet, and Lisa, our Portuguese housekeeper, is standing close holding Gus. We are waving at Mum out in the street. She is rushing to meet my dad. She is going to a party and she looks beautiful. When I grow up, I hope I run like that, taking swift elegant steps that don't ruffle you up or make you look at all messy. She waves back at us and then she falls. Lisa yelps and hands Gus to me and before I can even take a new breath, she has flown out of the house and gathered up my mum. Mum stays only long enough to have her knee bathed and change stockings and laugh in a breezy way and tickle me in the neck. There was blood, though, and I wrote it down in the casebook. She bleeds.

But this is different.

Ben is coming up the stairs, moving quickly, and he looks pretty serious like he knows exactly what is going on and suddenly he is right behind me, crooking one long arm loosely around my neck, pulling me back a bit, because I am standing in the path of these men who are taking my mother away. She turns her head in my direction and extends one arm, waving her long fingers in that way she has, and smiling, although all this looks a little hard for her, she does it all a bit slowly and her eyes look like glass with rain on it.

"It's okay, Jem. You be a good girl, you do your homework." Her voice is quiet.

When I look at her moving past me on the stretcher, I know at once that the white hart in that Diptych painting, with Richard II on the other side, the white hart reminds me of her, that's who.

"Yes, Mummy." This is all I can say to her and I can tell that although my mother is smiling and stretching out her hand and speaking normal words, she feels different, and maybe wants to say other things to me. And I am standing still, mumbling "yes, Mummy," but I want to run after her and scream at the men who are on the landing now, and almost downstairs, I want to stop this thing altogether, I want it not to be going on at all, and it's so noisy within, this is the worst thing I have ever seen.

Ben says, "You want to come in our room? You can get up on my bunk."

This is a good invitation. You have to be specially invited to go in the boys' room and sometimes I even get to sleep in there with Jude if Ben is staying at a friend's house. I have to sleep on the top bunk because once when I was down below I got my hair all caught up in the metal webbing underneath the top bed and Dad had to cut me loose with scissors. When Jude and I are in the bunks we are pretty active, as the bunk is a submarine in World War II prowling for German U-boats and it is easy to get your hair tangled up if it is long, like mine, and you are doing a lot of marine activity.

I climb up on Ben's bunk and look around the room just below the ceiling at the prints of old railway carriages and engines. Locomotives. I love these. I follow them around the room and start all over again so I don't start crying. Ben is shuffling his school stuff around and Jude must have slipped in some time because now he is halfway up the ladder holding an entire packet of Rowntree's fruit gums, which I like a lot. He tears the packet carefully, making an incision with his thumbnail and hands me half. Red fruit gums are best and I'll even eat one if it is loose in my pocket and has fluff stuck to it.

Jude says, "I'll save you my red ones," and he goes down the ladder.

Now I really feel like crying and I curl up, with the fruit gums in my left hand and my right hand between my face and Ben's pillow, so I don't get it wet. I don't make much noise at all.

Twenty-eight years on, the problem of fallibility in an angel or spirit, or a good witch, does not bother me at all because I understand it differently now. It's a habitat thing. You watch a lion or a gazelle in a zoo and you are not getting the full picture; you are seeing the behavior of a lion or a gazelle in captivity. This is what I've learned about spirits who have gone walkabout on earth. You have to make provisions so they can survive. This is what I would write in my casebook if I still had it. I don't need it, though, I've made my case and I have no doubts about my mother. I know what she is.

My mother likes champagne and she likes meursault. Quite early on in life I saw how good these drinks were for her and I aimed always to have enough money so that these wines lurked in my fridge, in case she breezed by wherever I happened to be living as a full-grown person with a life of my own. I think at heart, angels are party creatures and I am confirmed in this every time I go to the National Gallery and check out the Wilton Diptych girls, hanging around in languorous poses, willowy limbs draped over and through each other, biding time, their minds on festivity. These are party girls, and like the angels in other pictures, the huffing and puffing ones in rosy T-shirts in *The Dead Christ Supported* by Bellini; even the very beautiful Gabriel in Filippo Lippi's *Annunciation*, an angel with impeccable manners giving the big news to Mary, who will clearly have fewer and fewer free nights to read in bed, which is what she was doing before Gabriel arrived holding up two delicate fingers indicating the dual nature of Christ, human and divine. Yes, for all these angels, attending ceremonies, hauling up expiring saints to heaven, delivering big news from above, this is just the day job. The day job is very tense and demands physical strength, mental circumspection, and refined behavior. The desire to party is a simple need, that's all.

These are the provisions we all have to make for my mother, because if we do not pay attention, I will notice in her a sort of lonely, startled and wayward look, like in a lost animal or maybe a thirsty plant, and these are definitely wrenching sights to behold, and you have to arrest things before it is too late. There is not a lot to remember.

1. Champagne and meursault of fine quality.
2. Art, especially paintings featuring her friends and also strange abstract ones. Maybe they look like home to her, I don't know.
3. Beauty. Keep her away from bad architecture, ugly streets, asymmetry and brash noises. This is sometimes hard to do, but prolonged exposure to any of this has a marked effect on her, so this provision requires extreme vigilance. Starry skies are very good for her, as I have shown. She has friends up there.
4. Thoughtfulness. Please beware the careless remark and the rash gesture. These are killers. Spirit poison.

Snow is bluish, pinkish, sparkling, muddy, and looks different according to the light, sun or gloom, moonlight, lamplight, no light, but hair is never white as snow. That is fairy-tale stuff, a soft shoe idea, not real. My mother's white hair has gray in it, black, a trace of yellow, and a bright white streak where it was always so, even when the rest was black, just like Cruella De Vil, as Ben dreamt. I am stroking it now, away from her temples, and I remember my favorite story from her childhood, when she looked in a magazine and admired the ladies within, making beauty preparations. My mother thought she would do the same and she stepped out onto the balcony of the cold-water flat she lived in and cut off her beautiful curls. She was going to a party. And when she grew up, she became a fashion model, a star, a girl frozen in a party state. She is on her way to a party, she is there, she is leaving. This is the kind of job spirits do when they come down to us.

I stroke my mother's hair as she lies curled up on her bed and I watch her tears flow and I wipe them away now and again, as gently as possible. It is like watching a foreign film wherein emotion is played out in real time and therefore has an effect of suspended time and fearful intimacy. You have to watch the whole scene, not just a pretty flash of teary eye, and it can be quite terrible, like you have never seen tears before. It can take a while, too, starting and stopping very quietly, like in my mother's case, and I will wait it out because it is down to me. I forgot about provision number four.

There is another painting I really like. It hangs right across the arch from the Filippo Lippi *Annunciation*. It is also by Filippo Lippi and is called *Seven Saints* and the impression I have is of seven guys having a chin-wag at a bus stop but they are all a bit distracted and looking off in various directions or at a saint who is looking at some other saint, or talking to no one, eyes skybound. John the Baptist is in the middle between Cosmas and Damion, the physician saints, who are both ignoring John and madly praying. Most of the guys are pictured with the symbols of their martyrdom and Peter Martyr is my favorite. He is looking really bored and is resting his head in his hand while Anthony Abbot chats him up and right in the middle of Peter's head, like it is a plate of dessert, is a big knife. Bloody, he is thinking, look at me now. Francis with gold stigmata is staring at him, oblivious to Lawrence, who is trying to get his attention. Lawrence is painted leaning casually on the grill on which he was martyred. It's a very weird picture and I place my mother in it. The guys would have to scoot up on the bench and I think they could use her company. Mum would be pictured with all of us on her knee, my Dad, Ben, Jude, me, Harriet and Gus, but she would be smiling that smile.

I have been going through dark times and making angry meticulous incisions on my wrists with large, sharp knives and my mother wants to know why. She is deeply hurt like I have cut her up, and not me. She is outraged. Why, she asks. Why.

And I could not answer, I could not tell her that part of this has to do with things I cannot control and do not understand, like her growing old and leaving us one day, rejoining the party spirits, making her one selfish move, her single ungenerous act, an unthinkable gesture I will find so hard to forgive. So if I get there first, maybe it won't be so hard. I won't be left at all. Instead the door opens and she'll be fashionably late, and she'll head straight for me, and there will be fine wine.

Meanwhile, I'm still here, and I am stroking tears away. It's all I can do.

RUNNING TIME

I have just seen a film which I think is pretty important viewing if
you are inclined toward a love encounter with a person who is not
a member of your family. Most people are, including some nuns I
have known.

This is the name of the film. *Un homme et une femme.* Claude
Lelouch made it in 1966 when I was four years old going on five,
and it won Best Film at the Cannes Film Festival and Best Foreign
Film at the Academy Awards. It was shot in black-and-white and
color and this was a little bit trend-setting, although the reason it
was in black-and-white and color is that Claude ran out of money
and could not afford all color stock. This goes to show how acci-

dents can be fortuitous, like the Tarte Tatin story, for people interested in sweets and culinary tales.

I don't believe if you are a girl that you can watch this film and
not want to be Anouk Aimée and have the kind of moment she
has on the beach when Jean-Louis Trintignant flashes the head-
lights of his muddy rally car at her and they race toward each
other and he twirls her all around even though she is a lot taller
than him, and their little kids are playing together and then there
is that Francis Lai tune and a very lengthy shot of a dog gambol-
ing on the shore. The tune goes: La la la la-la-la-la-la, la-la-la-la-la,
La la la . . . etc., and it is exceedingly poignant despite being a
little bit breezy, which is a French paradox, one of many. There is
an even better moment, though, and that is when Jean-Louis, also
called Jean-Louis in the film, walks toward Anouk at the end of
the story, catching her as she is about to change trains and just
when she realizes, yes, she does love him. Where is he? There he
is. La la la . . . la-la-la-la-la. Jean-Louis does an awful lot of racing
around in his muddy rally car to find Anouk, and if you are
Anouk, this must be a pretty fine feeling and it is one all girls look
out for. Here are some reasons why.

Jean-Louis and Anouk meet in Deauville, where Jean-Louis has
a little son and Anouk has a little girl at boarding school, and they
are single parents visiting their little kids and Anouk misses her
train so Jean-Louis, who is a racing driver, gives her a lift back to
Paris. Okay.

Anouk's husband is dead. She is a script-girl and he was a
stuntman, and I must say that the flashback showing how he died
in an on-set explosion is slightly hilarious because this man strikes
me as very annoying. He was the type of Frenchman with enthu-

siasms, and despite pony rides in exotic places, rolls in the snow and shoreline dinners with lots of amorous nuzzling, he liked to talk about his enthusiasms—the philosophy of samba is one particularly horrible one—and play some hideous tunes on the guitar. This is very French and goes some way toward explaining why they are prone to rash behavior and do all this racing around in love situations. They simply lose track of time, due to all this theorizing and talking about their enthusiasms. Mr. Anouk is the kind of man who would do a film shoot in remote Africa and come home to fill Anouk's chic flat with African masks and books on tribal lore. It would be very irritating, but she fell for him, and for me this is the interesting human flaw she has.

After the ecstatic twirling around on the gloomy beach in Deauville, Jean-Louis and Anouk dump the kids back at school and have a languorous sex scene in a hotel room. Suddenly Anouk gets an anxious expression involving knitted brows and a distant gaze, right while she is in the loving grip of Jean-Louis. She is thinking about the stuntman, about rolls in the snow, rides in open-top cars and speeches about samba. Not only that, we get to hear eighty-two verses sung by the stuntman, a gruesome ditty, wherein the main point is this. You will always be in my love shadow. That is definitely one way to ruin a person's life if you are aiming to get blown up on a film set. Pretty soon Jean-Louis is aware things are not okay and there is a very depressing scene of Jean-Louis and Anouk fully dressed, lighting cigarettes, calling for the bill and the train schedule on the hotel phone, and then Jean-Louis drives Anouk to the station. She cannot even drive in his rally car back to Paris. Of course not. Because here is Anouk's problem. The stuntman conveniently died before she could compare the living racing driver with him or before she could entertain the possibility of falling out of love with samba and speeches about tribal lore and the awful strumming of the stuntman's guitar. She has to love him even more now than maybe she ever did, and that is one of the problems with the expiring of loved ones when you are in your prime.

Jean-Louis had a wife, too. I don't think she was entirely well. Just before he is about to race she calls him up and tells him how she will always be with him, meanwhile hauling on a cigarette and looking a bit edgy. Jean-Louis on the other end of the phone seems a bit perturbed. No wonder he has a smash-up and ends up in a coma. What the doctors tell her is too much for Mme Jean-Louis and she starts to flee down the hospital corridor. Cut to radio announcer saying that Mme Jean-Louis Duruc took her own life in a fit of despair. I hate to say it but I think she was headed there anyway, coma or no coma for Jean-Louis. And this is his problem—living with the crazy move his wife made when he was just about to pop out of his coma, and now he can't even admit to himself that maybe he was falling out of love with this edgy, needy woman, no, not until Anouk comes along.

Now Jean-Louis is asking himself some life questions and having a crisis. I'll never understand women. What should I have done differently. The stuntman would have written and sung some awful song about this, which is one reason I like the racing driver a lot better. Jean-Louis wonders where he went wrong and why people can't let themselves be happy and now he is doing what he does best, leaping into a muddy rally car, racing around on roads, reaching the train station where Anouk, he knows, will be changing trains. La la la . . . la-la-la-la-la, la-la-la-la-la, La la la, etc. It's a pretty fine moment but it would not have been without the depressing scene in the hotel room where Anouk and Jean-Louis suddenly think about death and lose all their impulses for rushing toward each other and twirling about on beaches despite their mismatched heights.

I am glad I am watching this film when I can grasp the dark side, because this is often necessary if you want to be fit for the love encounter with a person not a member of your family.

Here is another reason I like Jean-Louis much more than the stuntman. He reminds me of Jude.

I am having a conversation with Jude. I am sitting on the floor of the room he shares with Gus, with my back against the door that connects his bedroom with the bathroom.

Jude is in the bath and I am telling him a story about the nun who vanished from my French convent. The vanishing nun. We are not allowed to talk about her at school and we all know she left the convent for love and sex. She was there and now she is not, and she broke her vows with Dieu and it's not a popular subject amongst the nuns at my convent. They are Italian nuns and smell of espresso and they are prone to fits of temperament in that Italian fashion. It's not always wise to bring up unpopular subjects with them but I do because that is the kind of crazy kid I am. I am a good student and I am in the glamorous group and we are allowed to behave a little bit badly because nuns are pushovers for glamour.

I say to Soeur Lucia, "Well, how is Soeur Mariella? When is she coming back?"

Soeur Lucia scowls at me in an irascible Italian fashion.

Soeur Mariella was the uniform nun. She did a lot of measuring up of girls for uniforms, then she'd order the right sizes and fit you. It was a weird system which no longer operates now that Soeur Mariella has vanished, but it made me wonder about nuns. We were the only school with this weird uniform system. Why didn't they have a contract with a school outfitter's like every other posh school and skip all this private fitting business? Nuns, you would think, leave the world partly because it is all a bit complicated, then they go and make things even more complicated. They have a lot to learn.

Soeur Mariella was jumpy and smiling, always swishing by quick sticks and cracking jokes and poking girls in the ribs. She heard a lot of stuff about the outside world from us due to her nature, plus the fact that girls are quite forthcoming in the process of being measured up. Soeur Mariella was so high all the time she made you feel you had to get busy doing things, especially if you were in a bad mood before she came swishing by. Who is she with out there? Maybe a tailor, a tailor who is now always in the mood to get busy because of Soeur Mariella. The girls miss her around here. We hope she is doing okay. She should send us a message, she really should.

Jude likes this story, which I have told him a few times by now with ever more elaborate speculation and bold unfounded detail. It appeals to him, this story about a nun on the loose.

"What did she look like?" he asks.

"Cool!" I say. "A bit like . . . ahh . . . um . . . you know, in *The Railway Children*."

"Jenny Agutter!"

I only pretend to forget her name so as not to be too obvious. Jude is crazy for Jenny Agutter in *The Railway Children*. I'd never forget her name. Actually, Soeur Mariella in no way looks like Jenny Agutter, as Soeur Mariella is a southern Italian. She had dark hair, as far as I could tell from the wisps escaping her head-dress or whatever, but that is it. Never mind. Jude is crazy for Jenny Agutter and is therefore not thinking straight. He knows all the nuns at my school are Italian.

Jude has a date tonight and he will be some time in the bath even though he is supposed to be cooking dinner for us because Mum and Dad are going out this evening. Ben will be in charge when Jude goes out. It will be fun. Ben is really good at making up games. I wish Jude were not going on a date tonight as we could all play Creepy in the Dark, if Harriet does not lose her mind, that is. Harriet is three years younger than I am and sometimes it seems like a very great big span of time, like a century almost. Creepy in the Dark involves turning all the lights off and hiding and slithering around in a deathly quiet manner and ambushing a person, going in for the kill. There aren't really any winners and it is very exhausting and kind of bloody, without real blood of course, unless one of us bashes into a piece of furniture or some-thing. It's a game that can make you very edgy, and Harriet usually cracks up first. Harriet is always keen to play, but then she loses her mind due to fright and excitement. It's a problem.

"Gus is going to get really hungry if you don't hurry up," I say. Gus is only six.

"Yeh-yeh."

Before his bath, Jude took a quick shower and washed his hair. He has a shower before a bath ever since he heard Mum explain that's what Japanese people do, considering it quite disgusting how we in the West just rise up right out of a bath and that's it, we're clean. We should shower straight off. Otherwise, apparently, we are just all covered up in our own dirt still. It's quite a disturbing thought and sometimes I wish Mum had not told us this story. She knows a lot of stuff about Japanese people. In the war comics I still read, *Victor, Valiant, Commando, Tiger,* Japanese are called rice noshers by British soldiers. They say this in exasperated tones, clambering around in the heat, oppressed by wartime tension and extremes of temperature. It's forgivable. My dad says "Nips" sometimes, just to outrage Mum, who goes along with it and exclaims "Oh, darling!", but actually she is smiling that smile of hers which gives everyone a pretty warm feeling. She is getting ready to go out right now. Maybe my dad will let me bring her a glass of white wine soon. I like to do that. So does Jude, but he is in the bath, doing date preparations.

I hear a splash.

"Fuck!" says Jude. Jude is fifteen and he is into swearing, but it never sounds natural, not to me, anyway.

"That is a very boring swear word. Do you know what fuck means?" I ask through the bathroom door, repeating some words of Mum's who only ever says "Oh dear" or "Jiminy" or something like that when really annoyed.

"Jem, go away!"

"Jude?"

"What!"

"Rule number 8. Never read a book in the bath. It will always fall in. . . . Is that one of Dad's books? It better not be. Jude?"

"Yeh," he says, pretty quiet. It must have been one of Dad's books.

"I'll help you with supper, okay?"

"Okay."

When Jude comes downstairs he has his woolen ski cap on and he looks like a World War II British commando. I am cutting up vegetables, celery, carrots, cucumber, so that Mum can see we are having good nutrients and can go to her cocktail party and dinner with Dad, all relieved on the subject of nutrient intake going on at home amongst her kids. I will have to cut up a lot of cucumber due to Gus, who can eat just about a whole cucumber without blinking. He definitely has a big thing for cucumber. I glance at Jude but make sure not to include his commando hat in my scope. I do not want to make him self-conscious. He wears this cap to flatten his curls after hair washing because he thinks girls see curls as a bit sissy in a boy. Personally, I like Jude's curls and the poetic look they give him. I like this better than his hair all flat on top with a lot of it dangling over his eyes, the ends gradually curling up. I like to see his eyes. But I am only his sister and I guess it shouldn't really matter to me.

Jude doesn't say anything and opens up the fridge, hauling out hot-dog packets and cheddar. He is going to make curly dogs with cheese, his invention. Standing in the open fridge, he grabs the grapefruit-juice carton and looks swiftly over each shoulder, like he is a spy in a spy film. We are not supposed to drink straight from the carton.

"I'll cover you," I say, brandishing my knife and standing back to back with him, assuming a vigilant expression.

Jude puts the juice back and gathers up the stuff he needs, board and knife and hot dogs and cheese, and flaps about like he needs all the space in the world, jostling me and elbowing me and shoving me over with his hip just for fun. Then he does his Moby Dick impression, rising up and leaning forward as if riding a wave, his head rigid but the eyeballs swiveling slowly in my direction. I love his Moby Dick impression. I wish he were staying in with us. We could watch *The Hound of the Baskervilles*, which I happen to know is on later. We could watch with Ben when Harriet and Gus are in bed. Oh well.

These are Jude's curly dogs with cheese: make about seven slits all down the hot dog widthways but do not cut right through the hot dog. Cut up cheddar or some other nice cheese such as gruyère. Sauté up the hot dog and watch it curl up, making it a curly dog. Let the skin get quite crispy, which is best for contrast between the inside and outside. Carefully lay cheese on top until it is melty. Eat with mustard or ketchup, or alternate bite by bite. It is pretty good, and I can easily eat two, sometimes three curly dogs with cheese. So can Gus, which is quite surprising seeing as he is very thin and only six. Gus eats slowly and steadily with great concentration and graceful manners. I have never seen so much food go into such a small human being, and I watch him with furtive fascination and wonder if it will always be like that with him.

Dad saunters in and he is all dressed up, meaning he is wearing a white shirt with the collar done up and a tie holding everything together very neatly. He is wearing a dark suit and he is drinking some single malt Scotch whisky. It always surprises me to see him dressed up like a character in a foreign film because usually he hangs around the place in a T-shirt and loose trousers and maybe a V-neck sweater with holes in it. Actually he looks really good, and I like that even in a suit he seems a bit messy due to his hair, which is kind of unruly and which he never combs. I do not think he even knows how to use a comb. I saw him pick one up once and look at it strangely and swipe it across his head, breaking it in half, with one piece flying up in the air and hitting the floor. That might have been the last time he tried. I see him now and think, hey, he looks fine. I feel proud. That is my dad.

Right now he has that expression on his face. He is about to make a crack or two and he is aiming for Jude. He has a few minutes to kill waiting for Mum, so it is time for some cracks.

"Is it snowing in here? Ha ha ha ha!" says Dad.

It's kind of lame. Jude and I roll our eyes.

"So. Big date, Jude? Taking your girl for a soda? Ha ha ha ha!"

When Dad went on dates, many many moons ago, he would go to what was called a soda fountain and buy a soda for his girl, which I take it is some kind of ice cream drink, and it would cost about two cents. Or they might see a movie with trailers and eat ice cream. That would also cost about two cents. We hear about this quite a lot. It all sounds a bit gruesome. And the whole two-cents business is pretty boring, too. Currency fluctuations and inflation have nothing to do with us. A long time ago, societies operated according to a barter system. Not all that long ago there wasn't any electricity. Maybe next time Dad brings up the two-cents business, I'll try this out on him. Maybe not.

Here comes Harriet and she has Mum on the end of her little hand. She has a beaming expression, like she made Mum all by herself and wants everyone to see her fine work. And it is fine work. I can't help it. I am just crazy about this woman. Whenever I see her, I get this pain. It's not a bad pain, just a prickly feeling like I am all of a sudden aware of my heart—its shape, the size of it, the two ventricles, the pumping action, the vulnerable little veins running across it and the arteries leading in and out. It's weird.

We all pause for a second and take a look at Mum and she smiles that smile as if to say, what is all the fuss about, what is going on here?

Everyone bustles about, Gus wandering in looking thoughtful, Ben appearing from the basement, there is a lot of kissing going on between Mum and her kids and talk about bedtime and not leaving all our homework for Sunday and so on, and then Harriet dances Mum to the door and out, and Gus and I watch from the study window and I hike him up a bit so he can wave at Mum. Dad is not into waving. We don't expect him to, we don't need waves from him. Okay. So that's one date on the road. An hour or so until Jude's gets under way. Gus escorts me to the kitchen. He is hungry.

So is Harriet, who enters by way of jetés. She hardly ever moves in a regular fashion. Sometimes it is a bit much, her legs whipping in the air when you are trying to watch TV, or she comes crashing right into you when you are walking into a room she is flying out of. Her big thing for movement can pose problems. A bit like her way with food. She is trying to change her ways, but it is hard going. There will be trouble with the curly-dogs situation and I try to prepare her. Harriet is not keen on her foodstuffs touching each other on a plate. She likes to eat each item separately, i.e., not touching. She has a worried look as she comes up behind Jude, trying to peek at what is going on in the frying pan.

"Harriet," I say. "Help me with the table."

"Okay."

"Harriet. Let me tell you something about curly dogs with cheese. This is how it is. They are one item. A curly dog with cheese is one idea. It looks like it is two things touching but it only exists as a single thing, you see? It's not really touching at all. You like butter, right? Well, it's like toast with butter. You cannot have them apart."

"I see," she says, and she stops biting her lip. I can tell the buttered-toast thing worked.

Supper goes well and Jude gives Gus a burping lesson and Ben plays some weird music, which we all say is really cool, except for

Harriet, who claps her hands to her ears like she is in a lot of pain. Playing music loudly upstairs is something we only do when my dad is far from the house, so the strangeness is kind of a holiday, and we like to learn new things from Ben, so we let him play us whatever he wants. It makes him happy.

The back door bell rings. Jude's date is here.

Jude jumps up, whipping his commando hat off. "Jem, get the door!"

"Why me?" I don't budge.

"Just go!"

Ben goes to the door and Jude races upstairs to finish off his preparations, brushing teeth and so on. Mum says "ablutions." It's a good word. Jude's date steps into the kitchen with a really big smile and right off I don't like her at all.

"Hi, I'm Gabrielle!"

Yuck. I nod at her, pursing my mouth a little and say "Hey" without a lot of energy. Ben offers juice very politely and Gus pays no attention at all, he is still busy with his last curly dog with cheese. Harriet swivels in double-quick time and grips the back of her chair.

"Hello!" she announces in a really strange way, like a television newscaster. "Jude is not here!" Then she swivels back around and fiddles with the rest of her curly dog, muttering, "Where is Jude Weiss?" and "Who is that? What is going on here?" She keeps saying this, trying out different intonations, looking at me and back to her plate and giggling. It's a bit weird but I am enjoying it, and although I should probably tell her to stop being weird, I let her carry on. Ben bustles about with crockery and talks about anything just to drown her out, then Jude appears, his hair kind of flat and with his favorite jeans on.

Gabrielle strikes me as too neat. Her hair is really short and neat and she has a V-neck sweater on and jeans with an ironed crease in them. Very uncool. Also, her perfume is so poxy, it is bigger than the curly dog with cheese smell, which I like a lot better. A lot better.

Gabrielle has something for us and she hands it to me, because I am a girl. So is Harriet, but she is not so obviously in command of her mental faculties. Gabrielle hands over a huge flat plastic container.

"Dessert! It's mille-feuille. I made it for you."

I feel like Harriet. I want to say, what's going on here? But I thank her instead, as if mille-feuille is just what everyone here wants. First of all, no one makes mille-feuille, especially in a gigantic gruesome slab like this. Mille-feuille is made by French people, generally pastry chefs at French pâtisseries, and they make it in small pieces served delicately in a little paper thing with creasy pleats in it. We don't have a big thing for puddings anyway, except Mum's applecake or cheese pie, which are extremely, extremely good. Why is the date cooking about an acre of mille-feuille for kids she doesn't even know? What does she aim to do with Jude? This is a bribe, and I don't like it. I want Jude to see I don't like it but he is pulling on his coat, eager to be out of here. Gabrielle does up the buttons of her really neat duffel coat. She is so neat I feel like a wild woman or an animal on the loose.

"Are we still going to see *The Sting* tomorrow?" I ask him, trying to act like I don't care if he has changed his mind but coming off a bit pathetic anyway, a feeling that makes me jump up with my plate and start clearing the table.

"Yeah, sure," he says, a bit shifty. It's not a warm voice. It doesn't sound like Jude and I have butterflies in my stomach and a lump in my throat. I don't care. Maybe I won't want to go with him tomorrow, maybe I'll go out early when he's still asleep, and pretend I forgot.

He says "Bye" into the kitchen, not looking at me. Then he is gone.

I wonder about Gabrielle. I wonder if he first saw her at a dance, like in *West Side Story*, and when they spotted each other, everything around them went silent and there was only them noticing each other and having an epiphany or something. It's such an amazing moment, they have to sing. I like musicals, especially *West Side Story* and *Oliver!* but I am confused by them. Do the characters know they are singing at each other? Or are they supposed to be carrying on talking but the feeling is so special that in their imagination, it just has to be a song, simple speech no longer enough for them? That's what it must be, because otherwise, where does the music come from? Are orchestras following them around in case they feel a song coming on? It doesn't make sense. It's a magic thing, like slow motion and flashbacks and dreams in films. You can do a lot in films but it is not real. For instance, Tony and Maria spotting each other and the world goes quiet. This is called "pas de deux" in the musical.

Tony: You're not thinking I'm someone else?
Maria: I know you are not.
Tony: Or that we've met before?
Maria: I know we have not.
Tony: I felt—I knew something never before was going to happen—but this is so much more—
Maria: My hands are so cold. Yours too. So warm.

Tony: So beautiful.
Maria: Beautiful.

I can't connect this scene with Jude and Gabrielle. No. Instead, I see Bill Sikes rising up out of bed like a beast, shouting, "Of course I do, I lives with ya, don' I!" when Nancy asks him if he loves her. He doesn't. Those are the facts. Then comes a very bad news event involving a walking stick and a lot of brutal strength and that is the end of Nancy. I try not to think about this, I try not to let my thoughts go this far, as far as the murder of someone you are supposed to love. But this I know. Gabrielle does not look like Jenny Agutter. Not in the slightest. And I am not putting that mille-feuille in the fridge. Forget it.

The Hound of the Baskervilles is definitely a spooky film. I would call it dark. In fact, Sherlock Holmes is pretty spooky himself, he has a dark mind, something you have to have in order to grasp the villainous mind, in order to be several swift steps ahead of it. If Sherlock were simply a handsome tall man with a pipe playing the violin, I do not think he would be a hero in the sleuthing world. He would just be a handsome tall man with a pipe playing the violin and not really getting anywhere. Instead, he goes in for cocaine and rash behavior, sharp mood swings and depressive episodes because he is attuned to the dark side and to villainy. This is how I see it.

We have turned all the lights off in the study for extra spook-power. Ben lets me scoot up next to him on the sofa, where we both sit with our knees just about right under our chins and now and again we fling our arms around each other for reassurance in the especially gruesome bits involving the tearing up of human beings by hounds. Why anyone would go walkabout on the moors in the dead of the night when there is a rumor about wild hounds is a question that does not arise. This is how it is in scary films. I am not sure I would scoot up next to Ben like this if Jude were watching with us, because he might think I was being a little bit sissy. I have that wrong. Ben would not scoot up right next to me if Jude were with us, because Jude would think Ben was being a bit sissy. It's possible he is, but this doesn't bother me at all. It doesn't bother me that I have to take care of him in some situations, no, it does not. If Ben sees blood, he is prone to fainting in a heap of long limbs right on the floor in front of you. That is, if he sees blood on another person. His own blood leads to delirium practically. He goes all white and trembly, even if he just has a little paper cut or something. There are two small problems due to Ben's fear of blood. (1) Ben is not much help in a blood situation. You will have to find someone else to gather you up and do some nursing. (2) If you are aiming for an accident and Ben is around, you have to have your wits about you and keep the worst from him, if you are still standing that is. Try not to let him see the gore. It will freak him out big time. It is interesting that Ben has a very big thing for horror and has what he calls a gothic imagination. There is an awful lot of blood in the fields of horror and the gothic imagination. Ben is complicated. I am crazy about him but I am very glad we do not live in wartime, wherein Ben might be called up for active duty and have to go in for hand-to-hand combat with guns and knives, inviting all kinds of blood situations. I am thankful for peace for this reason alone.

Just as the film is ending, with only the flickering light from the TV letting us know what's what and who we really are, there is a terrible rattle at the study window. If Ben and I were not respectively seventeen and fourteen years old and therefore equipped with pretty strong hearts and nerves not yet ravaged by artificial stimulants and full-blown grown-up emotions, we might have been felled by fear and had heart attacks right there on the sofa. As it is, we are quite rattled. It's only my dad, of course, and when he comes in the front door behind Mum, who is kind of glowing, he is very very pleased with himself and is shaking with mirth. His hair is wilder than when he left the house and his tie is loose around his neck. He still looks ace, though. I try not to seem as if I have recovered from the rattle at the window because I know he is just so happy to have spooked two of his kids so badly, and now he can go up to bed with his arms around Mum, his topmost favorite person in the world, feeling really great about himself. Good night, Dad. Anytime, Dad.

Ben and I have a debate and it goes like this. Seeing as we are both seriously spooked, we need to be escorted to bed. So I will watch him get in bed and turn off the light. Then he has to get up and do the same for me. Then I get out of bed and see him safely to his room. Then he has to make sure I settle in okay, and so on. It could go on all night, so we decide, now that we are fully awake, to check out the comestible situation in the kitchen and sort ourselves out with snacks, which is a very good idea for chasing away the spooks. Cheese and tomato bagels are just the thing, although Ben is sure to add something disgusting to his, which is a quirk he has. He ferrets out some anchovies and olives. I don't want to look.

We hear the outer door bang at the end of the kitchen. There is an outer screen door and an inner door and we never take off the screen door in the winter because our Dad has no idea how to do these things; he just stands around with a screwdriver or a hammer, the only tools he recognizes, and looks silly for a few minutes until Mum says, never mind, darling. Anyway, it has to be Jude at the door or someone breaking in or maybe a hound of the Baskervilles. Jude is a bit noisy when it comes to doors and he is the only Weiss still not accounted for at 12:40 A.M. The only Weiss still out there in the wild.

It's Jude. He is a bit drunk.

"Hey, Jude," Ben and I say.

"Are you sicky drunk or okay drunk?" I need to know in case we are in for a vomiting situation requiring buckets and mops and rags we'll never be able to use again. I need to know also whether it is safe to bite into my cheese and tomato bagel without having a barfy feeling myself.

"Okay drunk," Jude mumbles. "What are you guys having?"

Jude slings off his hat and coat and throws them on top of the pile in the vestibule. He kicks off his boots, too lazy to undo them, but it is an almighty struggle. He swears and huffs and falls over.

"Jude. Rule number twenty-seven. Always unlace tight boots. It is faster to get your feet out of them that way. Thank you."

"Jem. Rule number twenty-eight. Shut up." Jude then comes over to the table and grabs my bagel. No problem. I get up to make a new one.

"How was your date?" Ben asks.

"Fuck. What a bore. God! Bla bla bla. Shut up, shut up, shut up! Fuck."

I glance over at that stupid square meter of mille-feuille on the counter near the toaster and feel an opportunity coming on. I fish out some wooden spoons from the drawer and hand one each to the boys. I say, "Murder on the Orient Express."

We do this now and then, usually with Gus because he doesn't lose his mind like Harriet. Gus is very patient when it comes to torture, which will set him up well in life, I think. Gus will go far, I just know it. He will be a leader of men. With Gus we use pillows to hit him when we do "Murder on the Orient Express." This game is named after the murder scene, filmed in blue night light wherein a lot of posh shifty types, all very cross with the same man, take turns plunging a knife into his drugged body, wriggling it out a little at the end, not before calling out their particular grudge in unhappy tones. Okay.

I take the lid off the mille-feuille and assume a wide-eyed expression due to extreme feelings of revenge and spite. I raise both hands in a zombie-like fashion and prepare to stab the mille-feuille.

"This is for having a stupid neat hairdo!" I say and stab, taking a few trancelike steps away from the mille-feuille.

Jude says, "This is for wasting three weeks of my pocket money." He plunges his spoon in and moves away slowly, joining the queue.

"This is for the crease in your jeans," says Ben, stabbing.

My turn again. "This is for wearing stinky perfume."

"This is for your tiny little boobs!" says Jude, getting a bit too specific for me. Never mind. It will do him good.

"This is for bringing mille-feuille." Ben is very good at murderous expressions. It appeals to his gothic imagination, I believe. He really gets into this game. It may be time to stop. Besides, the mille-feuille is beginning to splatter everywhere. I decide to act super crazed on my next go and finish it off.

"This is for boring a Weiss!" I announce, and stab the cake about eighty-two times until Ben and Jude drag me off. We go back to our bagels peaceably, feeling much better.

There is a snack pause.

Then I try to ask Ben a question. I begin quite normally, no problem, but I can't get the words out.

"Ben, are you, do you still see, how is . . ." It's unbearable. I look at Jude and flutter the fingers of my one hand at the edge of my plate with bagel on it. Right away Jude huddles over and his shoulders are shaking. He knows exactly who I am trying to ask Ben about. Goldfinger. Ben doesn't know that we call his ex-girlfriend Goldfinger.

One day Ben emerged from the basement with a girl who did not seem all that used to regular conversation. Mum was making dinner and some of her kids were chatting away to her in the kitchen. As usual, Mum sensed a certain hopelessness in this girl and asked her if she wanted to stay for dinner. There was a pretty strong oh no feeling in the kitchen when she said "Yes, thank you." Oh no. I tried to feel like a good person. I imagined I was a nun and this girl came scraping at my door seeking succor. What can you do? You can't pick them. Mum has a sharp eye for strays, misfits and other sorry types and she is always ready with a few questions bound to make the sad type open up like a flower. She is ready with food and time and so on and she is so cool about it the person would never know she found their weak spot in about half a second, that she zeroed in on the heart of this person and spied a big empty space just crying out for someone like Mum. I once saw a big handsome heartthrob friend of Ben's respond to some remark or glancing touch of my mum's in greeting and he clutched her like a wounded bear or someone who had just been shot. I thought he'd never let go. Pretty embarrassing behavior in a heartthrob. The downside of having a mum with a sharp eye for sad types is having to eat dinner with sad types like this ex-girlfriend of Ben's. You have to keep a straight face and, in her case, make sure not to speak too fast or use words involving poly-syllables. Bloody. When she came to the table she slipped off her shoes, like this is what you do before dinner. And her toenails matched her fingernails. All painted gold. Dinner was tough. From then on, whenever Jude and I saw her, we launched into the tune from *Goldfinger* once she had slithered into the basement to see Ben, or they had walked out of the house together on a date.

I look at Jude tonight and we just have to do it for Ben. We have to do it with full Bond-girl sashaying moves, requiring extravagant hip swiveling and waving arms like they are pieces of seaweed in a fish tank, and wide open eyes, like deep thoughts are not your big thing in life. We start wary and get looser. It's pretty late at night. We let go.

"Gold-finger! She's a girl—a girl with the Midas touch—a spi-der's touch—such—a cold finger!—beckons you—to enter her web of sin—but don't go in!" We are definitely close to hysterical now.

Then Ben joins in. Cool.

"Golden words she will pour in your ear—but her lies can't dis-guise what you fear!—for a golden boy—knows when she's kissed him . . . it's the kiss of death—from Miss Gold-finger! Pretty boy—beware of this heart of gold—THIS HEART IS COLD!—She loves only gold— only gold—SHE LOVES GOLD!"

We dance around the kitchen in a crazed sashaying fashion and bump into each other and soon we are a heap of bodies with beery scents, and bagel with cheese and tomato, and anchovy and olive scents rising up into the air. We are kind of steamed up.

Ben says, "What about Speckhead?"

I giggle and snort. We are still on the floor.

"Jude, *you* know," I say. "Your girlfriend with the long hair and the tiny head. I was really worried about her. I didn't think there was room in there for all the things you need. Like a frontal lobe and so on." I am getting helpless with mirth and derision.

Jude lunges at me and hunkers down for the typewriter tickle, the worst of all. You pin the victim's arms close to his body and tap on the chest in a rapid typing motion. It's gruesome.

"Don't! I can't breathe! I'll throw up my bagel! I'm in puberty! Stop!"

Once in my dad's mum's house, she stopped me from moving an armchair, rushing up to me and waving her hands about. "Don't! You're in puberty!" she said.

I had no idea what she was talking about and asked Mum about it later. She and Dad exchanged weary looks. Dad's mum is thoroughly weird, but I say this all the time now. No, I can't set the table, I'm in puberty. No, I can't do the washing-up this evening, I'm in serious puberty, etc.

Jude rolls off me and we all catch our breath. We take a rest from mirth.

"Didn't Mum look great tonight," I say into the ceiling.

There is stillness in the kitchen while we all have our separate thoughts about Mum and how she looked, and other stuff too maybe, like how she is kind of all ours but not, how she is apart, in some private place. Never mind.

"She always looks fucking great," says Jude.

"Yeh," says Ben.

"Jude, do you know what fuck means? Jude—"

"Jem, rule number twenty-eight!"

"Shut up?"

"Right."

It's time for bed. We shuffle our mess away, not talking, working smoothly together, a little tired now, thinking about tomorrow, a day we are already in. Soon we are trooping upstairs, turning lights off and patting each other on the shoulders, whispering good nights, a bit shy and formal but tight as musketeers.

I lie awake for some time. I'm not sleepy and it's strange, because I think about sad things, even though I am feeling really good and have a fluttery sensation in my stomach which comes with high times. I remember when Jude fell off a wall and Ben had to overcome his fear of blood situations because we were little kids then and he was the oldest and there were no grown-ups around. I think of the time I watched Mum slip in the street running for a cab and waving back at us in the house; and the time Dad's great friend died and he tried to explain it to us when really there is nothing to explain at all, and I recall how most of the evening he just sat in the living room with his glass of Scotch whisky and stared straight ahead, not even knowing which one of us was saying good night to him. I think of Harriet when she was only four and I dropped her off at her classroom on her first day at my school and how her mouth went all wiggly at the corners and her eyes filled up with tears and she looked back at me like I had betrayed her, sold her into slavery or something. I think of all these things and I feel like I should have done something in all these situations, like I could have changed them somehow, made them come out better.

I am going on a date with Jude tonight. I have not seen him for nearly eight months and he is breezing through town, taking a few days off between jaunts in war-torn countries where he spends a lot of time walking around in his thoughtful, unhurried fashion, talking to war-torn people, even as bullets fly, threatening all life-forms. People respond to him and are willing with the kind of information they would not give up to the more feverish and egomaniac type of journalist. I picture Jude often, eating strange food in people's homes, dancing with them, drinking a little too much, falling asleep on the floor, giving his things away, playing with their kids, coming home with stories that are more than news. That's my brother Jude, only fifteen months my senior, barely even a separate person from me, although so far away now so much of the time.

I have had to tell Jude over a crackling telephone line that I am not in great shape, that I am taking medication for a little while and will soon have a holiday in hospital just to see if it helps, that's all, not for long or anything, and I am checking in there myself, no handcuffs and jackets tied up the back, so don't worry about it, where are you taking me tonight?

I don't tell him that I have been playing with knives, that I have been making observations about their capacity to draw blood and etch fine lines on sensitive areas of the body without actually causing death. This would make Jude very crazy and speechless and jumpy and he really doesn't need to know. He doesn't need to know this also because I don't believe this is the real reason I need a holiday in hospital. There's another thing going on and it has to do with movies. I have an obsession at the moment with films involving love situations not involving a family member. I keep watching the same ones over and over again, because I am trying to understand why I won't get into this game myself, why it does not make sense to me at all. I keep looking for clues and loopholes in films and more and more I see the truth in them and realize I am right about the world, how it can never measure up. The spooky thing is, I have to watch the same film again and again because I have this fear that it changes when I am not looking. I sit really close to the TV and slip the film in the video and keep an eye out for change, from minor things like lighting to tilts of the head in close-up scenes, subtle costume alterations or a word missing from dialogue I know by heart, right up to big things like the outcome of events. I fear that bad situations will get worse and that fine moments never happened at all. It's making me crazy.

In *Jules et Jim*, François Truffaut 1961 1hr. 43min. 12sec., I feel for Catherine. Catherine goes all out for love but she is falling apart from the start. When she scoffs at German beer, she rattles off all the communes of Bordeaux and the vineyards of Burgundy and it is very charming, but the fact is, she is losing her mind and Jules et Jim should know this. I think they are worried, but they are helpless characters, they have never seen anyone like her. I watch the end again and again, because I need to make sure Catherine drives off the bridge taking only Jim with her to death. I have to check because I keep imagining Jules getting in the car too for a last ride. I can never be sure.

The thing about *On the Waterfront*, Elia Kazan 1954 1hr. 43min. 40sec., is how much you believe that Edie falls for Terry, that this fragile convent girl hell-bent on avenging her brother Joey, loves this puffy-eyed ex-prizefighter who has never read a book in his life but has some fine instincts and a tenderness of his own he finds easiest to express with pigeons. When Terry takes her for her first drink, he says all the wrong things, but you can see her loving him even though she tells him there isn't a spark of sentiment or romance or human kindness in his whole body. Just before getting up to leave, when he says he can't help her, she lays her hand on his cheek and you know this is the best thing that has ever happened to him. Their life together will not always be easy, but they have to go for it. I watch it again and again because it is possible Edie does not let him back into her life when she discovers how involved he was with the death of Joey. It is possible she took that bus ticket from her father and packed the bag and went back to the convent. I just don't know, and I need to keep checking that she sticks with him. Stick with Terry, Edie. Hold out for him.

This is why I take *Un homme et une femme* to heart, because even though it seems like one long jaunty ad for beach holidays, wine, cars, and cigarettes, it tells the truth about love situations. The twirl on the beach does not come easy, and there will be crack-ups, but I think they'll be okay in the end as long as they are prepared for drawbacks. I hope so.

So this is why I am taking a holiday. I am going to learn how to face up to drawbacks and maybe I will get my twirl on the beach with some type who is not at all my size.

I am waiting for Jude and I wonder if he has found his Jenny Agutter yet. I don't think so. I think I would know by now. *The Railway Children*, Lionel Jeffries 1970 1hr. 45min. approx. I have to be careful not to watch this one again and again because it gives me a terrible longing for things I cannot name. In the closing minutes of this film Jenny's father, a man with a friendly beard and fine posture, is released from prison. He has been falsely accused of treason. Everyone has seen the news, everyone except Jenny and they wave their papers at her, prodding at the headline as she stands on the railroad platform, her favorite place, and it is the right place at the right time, although she does not know that. When the London train screeches in and the carriage doors open, the world goes quiet. She makes him out in a cloud of steam and races his way, in slow motion and then real time. Daddy, my daddy. Pas de deux. A dance requiring perfect balance, no messing up.

Jude takes me to a funny Chinese restaurant with waiters dressed in what looks to me like Red Army uniforms but is supposed to suggest chic. There is a louche jazz band playing short sets of chintzy music. The only other diners strike me as confused out-of-towners and gangsters with molls. Jude says that actually the sax player is pretty good. Okay. Jude has no idea what to say to me but suddenly he gets up and tells me we will dance, because he feels sorry for the sax player who is pretty good and no one is dancing.

I cannot say no to Jude, I never can, but I am scared to dance. He holds my right hand in his left and my left shoulder in his right and I look over his shoulder and I crack jokes. The world does not go quiet, it gets noisy, very noisy, and I lose the ability to flex my joints, like the Tin Man in *The Wizard of Oz,* and I move my feet as if I am wearing snowshoes. It is awful and I want to run away from this awful date, but also I want Jude never to let go of me, ever, even though I know this is so hard for him and that being with war-torn people he barely knows in a place where bullets are a serious threat to all life-forms is a breeze compared to dancing with me on a night when I am not in the best shape, on a night I am such a mess that he is speechless with anger and fear.

Isn't it interesting, I think, that all war stories end up being about love. Of course, Jude has read them all.

SISTER CRAZY

We just moved to a new country. It's my dad's country, where he comes from, and our house is at the end of a street which is a cul-de-sac, a bum-of-the-bag as Jude likes to call it in select company. It's not poetic but these are the facts, cul-de-sac = bum-of-the-bag and frankly, this creases me up. It creases Ben up too. Harriet has no idea what we are talking about, but if her two big brothers and her one big sister are creasing up with mirth, she's likely to go for it too and start laughing in a big-hearted hysterical fashion, like she has just heard the funniest thing on earth.

So Jude saves this joke for us; he is pretty sure Mum and Dad will not find it very witty. It's hard to explain this kind of thing to our parents. Some things are just not worth going into, that's what you learn as you move along, and saying bum-of-the-bag is one of them. It strikes us as funny most of all when we are felled by kid-type pressures, for instance, we are lying around in a heap on the floor and it is late afternoon and flying through our heads are kid-type pressures like, bloody, I have a load of homework. And why does that weird kid follow me around at school. Or, will I get to watch the whole film tonight before Mum comes in and says "Bed-time." I know the first half of a lot of films by now and I am keen to see some endings, I really am. There are other pressures, like what shall I have for a snack and is there time for it between now and dinner, and what is this new country we are in and how long are we here for. When you are beset by worries like these, you get a bit weak, and if Jude then says let's go see what's up in the bum-of-the-bag, Jem, it's no wonder I crease up with mirth and get that helpless feeling.

The word bum is not a problem. You can say just about anything you like in our house as long as you know what you are talking about and you use your imagination. Otherwise, Mum and Dad are pretty quick to clear you up on the matter. Sometimes it is a good idea to check separately with each one of them if you want a fuller picture. If you want the bare facts about a word and it is not very likely to take up a large space in your regular vocabulary, you go see my dad. If you want some associated news, like images and ety-mology and poetic examples of usage of this word, you go to Mum. When Mum tells a story, I can just about sit there all day.

Harriet is a bit reckless when it comes to words, however. I keep telling her when she starts wandering around muttering some word to pass it by me first. If I don't know it and feel it may be a dodgy one, I'll take it to Ben, who is the oldest, and more pa-tient with research and dictionaries than I am. She won't listen, though. I believe there is a daredevil within. If this were an age before flight, my little sister Harriet would have been up there, the first woman, sitting bolt upright and gleeful in a rickety biplane with a leather flying hat on and a pair of goggles and maybe a long white scarf.

When Harriet feels the urge to test out a word she picks dinnertime. There she is, sitting up so straight her back is swaying in a little at her waist, she can't help it. She learns ballet and she takes this posture thing to heart. She thinks, Sit straight! Pile each vertebra right on top of one another, no messing up! She thinks it so hard, her little body seems electrified and she'll even look around at me or Jude if we are a bit slouchy due to the weight of kid-type pressures and give us a ballet-mistress glare of disapproval, involving a sharp turn of her head, a whip of blond ponytail and a wide-eyed expression. It can be annoying.

Then Harriet starts her muttering. She says something real quiet in between mini ballet-type bites of supper and she darts furtive looks in all directions and keeps repeating whatever she is saying in this little whisper, just inviting every single one of us to ask,

"Well, what is it, Harriet? What did you say? What's going on?"

"Fuck me," she says.

Oh-oh.

I am not surprised by my sister, not really, but Jude looks all around, waiting to see what will happen next, and Ben has a worried, responsible expression and fiddles with his cutlery, while Gus doesn't care because he is still a baby and is deeply involved with a crispy piece of potato. My dad bursts into hysterics and this is bad news for Harriet, who is going to cry any second now, her face starting to shimmer and break up. Then Mum smiles that smile and Harriet's eyes widen and she zooms in on Mum and her smile, just for some relief, and I understand this instinct of hers, this desire to shut out the whole world in a gruesome moment and latch on to Mum's smile.

I have examined this smile quite a bit, trying to see how it has the effect it does. Mum is very beautiful. It does not mean smiling has to be her thing. For instance, I have noted some women in old films who are beautiful and haven't the first idea about smiling and can look frankly terrifying or terrified themselves once they start moving the little muscles around the mouth and separating the lips. This woman Greta Garbo, for one. I watched her in a film called *Camille*, where she wore very big dresses and when she laughed and smiled at the man she loved, I thought, if I were him, I would run away or at least ask her if she was okay, did she need a glass of water or something. I really think there is some kind of art in the smiling and laughing business.

Sometimes I check myself out in the mirror and I note that I have a sort of lopsided thing going on when it comes to smiles. Also, the side of my mouth that wants to smile does not necessarily curl upward like it should but downward, which may be a little spooky for some observers. Most of all, I can be in company and have a big feeling for a smile but it just doesn't show up on my face. I am learning to make up for this so that even if I think I'm smiling like a clown in a circus, it's really only quite a normal-size smile. It's important to make these little adjustments when you get to know stuff about yourself. I frown a lot and not everybody likes this, but it is just that I have a lot to think about, a lot of things to work out, although now I try to be aware of my forehead and relax the muscles up there when there are a lot of people around, or even just Harriet, when we walk to school together. I know I am frowning if her head is hanging a little instead of being really perky. She bows her head and walks in front of me, or behind, and keeps checking my face and looking away, like she is some kind of small animal no one wants to play with. I have to watch out and be aware of things. It is more important to be careful when I am with Harriet because Harriet is my sister.

It makes me wonder though, what happens to a person's face— physiognomy is a word I heard from Ben—if they are crazy and have a lot of crazy thoughts and not much of an impulse to smile in a regular fashion. We saw this film once, *The Hunchback of Notre Dame*, which is a favorite film of my dad's of course, because there are a lot of crazy people in it, shouting and throwing things and looking in serious need of a bath. My dad loves films featuring this sort of person, he laughs and laughs. My dad loves this film so much that for about three weeks after we watched it, he escorted some of his kids to bed, loping behind us in the hall all hunched over and with a messed-up expression on his face, sometimes calling out "The bells, the bells." It was extremely annoying and I am glad no one from outside the family was around to see him during this three-week period.

In this film, Charles Laughton plays a hunchback called Quasi-modo, a name so strange and fun to say that Harriet spoke it about eighty-two times that night while I was trying to get to sleep.

"Quasi-modo," she says over and over, trying out a different emphasis now and then and finally sticking with one, which involves a slow, horror-movie type delivery of the first two syllables and a quick-fire pronunciation of the "modo" bit. It's working, because even though she acts like this is a game she is playing by herself and I am no part of it, she knows perfectly well it's getting to me, which is what this game is all about. Each time she says "modo" in that gunfire fashion, my heart starts jumping, although I know it's coming. I have to shout at Harriet to please shut up, despite the risk she will get horrible sulks and not talk to me the next morning, building a wall of cereal boxes or something between our places at breakfast so as not to see me. I will have to live with this possibility due to my need for sleep.

"Harriet! Stop it!" I rise up from bed and glare at her in the dark and she starts whimpering a little.

"Quasimodo," she says, turning over in bed and making a cave out of her sheets and blankets. "Quasimodo," she tries, one final time, in the quietest voice I ever heard. It's a bit heartbreaking. Harriet has a heartbreaking way about her.

I think some more about this film concerning a French hunchback in the Middle Ages. Quasimodo is pretty ugly. Is this the face of a crazy person whose thoughts are wild and do not come out right, like when you have had anesthetic at the dentist and you want to do things, say things, move your face a certain way, and it just does not happen? Then I saw that Quasimodo is probably not at all crazy, the least crazy one in the film. When he rescues the boring Gypsy woman, Esmeralda, and he has her all safe in his bell tower, he explains that although he cannot hear, he can understand sign language. Esmeralda has clearly not been to sign-language school or maybe it was not all that developed in the Middle Ages. She wants to know why Quasimodo rescued her and she repeats the question along with some sign language so he can understand. Her idea of sign language is to ask, "Why did you rescue me?" in words, and swish her hand with one pointed finger in front of her chest twice, depicting, I guess, her own self swinging on the rope Quasimodo rescued her on. To me it's not really enough, but Quasimodo says straight away, really calm,

"Why did I rescue you?"

Quasimodo is a smart guy and very sensitive. He can just about guess what you are saying even if you are hopeless at sign language. He is very ugly and sad but he is okay and not crazy, so I have decided that signs of craziness will not always show up in the face. In the physiognomy of a person. You have to look a lot closer than that. I am pretty sure there can be craziness lurking inside a person and it does not show up at all, and that in the same confusing manner, some signs of behavior look crazy but the person is not. My dad is a really good example of this.

When Harriet has said fuck me, at dinner, I understand the way she holds out for Mum's smile, how her big blue watering eyes just go all out for Mum in a desperate fashion. That smile of hers is really useful for solving problems and making you feel okay when you never thought you would again, but sometimes that smile can be pretty bloody. This is when. You rise up on a school morning and get very clean and even comb your hair until it flies around in a really stupid way and you barely recognize your own self in the mirror. You haul on your school uniform and it is stiff and refuses to fit your body right like your jeans do, and Jude's old rugby top from the country we lived in before, the top that is now too small for him and that you love wearing because it was his and still smells of him and of the country you lived in before. You do not want to go to school today, not in the least. What is the point. What is the point of anything.

"What's wrong, Jem?" Mum says although she does not sound all that worried. She is paying a lot of attention to Gus, our baby. She's on to me.

"I think I am sick," I say, speaking low and like words themselves are difficult to throw together into a sentence, like I could faint any second now. "I don't—I think—I might—maybe I should stay home today."

"Why don't you step outside first, and take some DEEP BREATHS!"

Then she smiles at me. She looks right at me and one eyebrow raises up a little and she smiles.

"Oh forget it," I say, a bit sharp and grumpy. "I'll go. Bloody." I don't even bother with the deep breaths business.

That is when Mum's smile is kind of crafty, making you do a thing you ought to be doing but definitely don't want to do.

It's too late for Harriet now, because Dad is laughing big time and he is drowning out Mum. Everyone perks up at the table and the ends of Harriet's mouth go all wiggly and here it comes, tears, lots of them.

You have to be really careful with laughter around my sister. She does not have a big thing for laughter even though she looks so merry, like everything in the world goes just right for her and she cannot understand why anyone could have a problem, which is why she looks so crushed if I am frowning on our way to school, why it is so scary for her, just like a big storm with lightning and thunder which is something else she cannot understand, the suddenness and angry noise of it, making her run around the house closing all the windows with great strength and decision even though she is such a small person, as if Harriet herself, my little sister with a big thing for dancing but not laughter, can hold off chaos all on her own, just by showing you how much it freaks her out, like that is enough.

It is enough for me. I stop frowning when I take note of her shivering small-beast expression. I let her close the windows of our room if the trees are too whooshy in the wind at night and she can't sleep, and I hate the windows to be shut at night. I let her, though.

And I understand her problem with laughs. I understood how it is for Harriet when I heard Greta Garbo in those films, it's the same thing, it can be a shock you feel right inside your body and all through it, as if someone you are crazy about turns around and hits you out of nowhere. It's a bad feeling.

I remember a birthday party for Harriet once, when she was a little kid, after the bit where all her chirping friends came and tossed balloons and wore little hats and separated smarties and other sweets into color codes and so on, clearly little kids quite like Harriet in some ways with a lot of peculiarities in their behavior, involving methodical reorganizing of their immediate surroundings. Nothing any one of those little kids did seemed to surprise any other kid. Okay. There was lots of chirping going on and it struck me they were like a row of starlings on a telephone wire, when they all sit squashed up together, usually late in the afternoon, like this is a really good time to meet and talk about their day all at once.

Maybe Harriet was a little tired after all that, but when it was time for grown-up dinner and we all sat together at the white oak table, which had been cleared of party stuff, it was soon time to bring on Harriet's cake so she could blow out her candles and then make the first cut, Mum holding her hand over Harriet's very small one grasping the knife like it was the weirdest most fearsome object she had ever held on to, and guiding her, the knife upside down for wish power. You close your eyes, you cut upside down slowly, in time with your wish that you make with your eyes closed, slowly, so you don't cut all the way through the cake and you are only about halfway into your wish. Ben, for instance, cuts real fast on his birthday and it is very aggravating to behold because I keep thinking he did not, he could not, have made his wish in that time and I worry he will lose out for a whole year. I can't help it. I worry about things like that.

Harriet, though, must make the longest wish in history because when she gets to the cutting bit, her eyes are squeezed tight and she cuts in slow motion, occasionally opening up her eyes and checking with Mum, and I know Harriet wants to tell her what she is wishing and I have an urge to warn her not to, because otherwise the wish will not work, but I do not need to as Harriet is well informed when it comes to all that stuff, magic and wishes and all types of things that are not everyday things, that are a bit weird. I am pretty sure she wishes something weird, too, like the power to fly or that all her stuffed animals would turn into real ones or that she could eat chocolate only, forever, at all mealtimes.

My sister loves chocolate and this is another weird thing, that on her birthday she asks for cheese pie. But cheese is not Harriet's thing. She has a big thing for chocolate, not cheese at all. I am the one with a big thing for cheese, but on my birthday I ask for another great cake of Mum's, a chocolate one with melted After Eight icing. It's a pretty cool cake but I wonder about it now, and I think that on our birthdays, it is as if my sister and I were standing face to face and my big thing became her big thing and hers became mine, just for these days, our separate birthdays, like a mirror game, a crazy-type mirror like the ones they have at fun fairs. One day when Harriet is bigger, I'll tell her this idea I had because I know she will like it, but she may be too young right now and get confused.

Before Harriet gets to cut upside down with Mum's hand over her own, she has to blow out the candles. This is what happens. We all huddle close to her and she sits up in that ballet way and takes in just about all the air available in the big kitchen and looks around for a second with that posh ballet expression on her face. She looks like a bird on a lawn with her chest all puffed up, she looks like a bird when it is gearing up for a song and you feel special watching, as if the tune coming soon were aimed at you, a message, an announcement. It's so funny seeing Harriet all poised to blow that we laugh. All of us. And Harriet deflates, a party balloon, and the edges of her mouth tremble and the tears come down. This is funny, too.

Laughter. Mum tries again, she has explained to Harriet over and over, this distinction, a word I like because it means different and special at the same time, she explains that there is a distinction between laughing at and laughing with. She gives examples, she explains it well, in the gentlest voice, so that you will not ever forget the meaning. When Mum explains a thing, you get this picture in your head and you don't ever need anyone to explain it again. That's how it is. But Harriet, she knows, is still not ready. She tries hard, I can see the thoughts moving around in her eyes, but I know for Harriet, just now in her life, what hits her first off is the sound, and she feels it physically and it hurts her, like she thinks we are laughing because she has done something crazy. You didn't, Harriet. You didn't.

I thought that maybe when Harriet hears laughter, it's like when a storm is coming and she wants to close all the windows because it's too noisy too quickly out there in the world.

I also looked up ear in my dad's encyclopedia, the big set Mum gave him one Christmas. There was a really good diagram in it and names of parts and little arrows and so on. The eardrum separates the outer ear from the middle ear, where three bones connect it to the inner ear. The inner ear has two things. One. The cochlea, which is responsible for balance and turns sound into nerve impulses. It tells Harriet's brain about her place in the world, the movements she is making. It must work really hard in Harriet and is maybe extremely sensitive due to her big thing for dance. Two. The hearing part, called the labyrinth. I looked up labyrinth: complicated structure with many passages hard to find way through or without guidance, maze. That's what I thought. It sounds like Harriet to me, she has a maze inside her. And this is what I worked out about Harriet soon after that birthday party.

So on the night my sister tries out her new expression, on the night she says fuck me, after a lot of the usual coaxing from everyone at the table, she cannot be saved by Mum's smile because of Dad and his kind of mountain-lion laugh, his shoulders and chest shaking like he is in a small car on a very bumpy road. My dad can't help it, having this laugh and being the biggest person in our family, and Harriet can't help crying and looking helpless like one of those dying ballerinas, all loose and in a heap but getting up about eight more times to do a few more steps, because dying is a really slow and delicate process for ballerinas, unlike for soldiers in war films, where one shot is usually enough to keep them lying down for good, no death throes at all.

Harriet has heard this new expression in my dad's country, but I don't know where. I have uneasy feelings about this new country, but most of all I worry about Harriet here, because she is not a suspicious type, she is really open and friendly and this place may be too big and too noisy. I am going to have to watch out for her even more than usual. That's my plan.

Harriet is not silly, she is open and friendly and I do not mean that she will go right up to a person and hang on to their cuff or anything, but if you are a stranger and you take a look at Harriet, she will have an open and friendly gaze, she will not frown and scare you off the way I do. Harriet is inviting and although that is a much nicer way to be than the way I am, it is not always safe. Next, Harriet has a habit of going astray, not quite lost, just sort of wandering free of you like a kite does in the air when it is first of all flapping and fighting in your arms and suddenly it's aloft and graceful and offering up some resistance, connected to you still but doing its own thing. I have noticed that when Mum is out with all her kids in a park or a museum or zoo or somewhere, she turns around at regular intervals, real cool though, not anxious or anything and not even searching Harriet out directly but she will say her name in a very soft fashion, "Harriet," she says just like that, as if Harriet were still right next to her, and I see that when Mum does this, Harriet moves in closer from wherever she is, she skips in toward us a little without joining us exactly. It is a bit like a homing signal for a bird and very reassuring.

I am not as calm as Mum. If I lose sight of Harriet I get cross with her because she has made me picture her at the bottom of an old pit or under a fallen tree or lost in a huddle of shops or having tea with a stranger, but usually I find her quite easily and she is perched on her little haunches talking to a bird or feeding a squirrel. She has a really big thing for animals and they have a really big thing for Harriet, kind of following her around like she is one of them. Sometimes I walk into our bedroom and she is sitting in the window and talking away merrily. You might think she is crazy, but she is not. She is having a conversation with a small animal who has come into the space she left by opening the window a little and they are having a snack together, sharing an apple or a nice roll with butter. It's weird in a good way, and I stay quiet, watching them. Harriet will never be alone, I think, not ever.

116

Fuck me, she said. Bloody.

Dad says to my sister, "It's okay, Harriet. It's not serious. I'll explain this word to you later, okay? We'll have talkies, how about that?" He wants her to stop crying. He feels bad.

Harriet takes in two sharp half-breaths and says, "O-kay," with another gulpy half-breath right in the middle. Then Dad tries to cheer her up and takes her plate and gets ready to serve her some more chicken and vegetables. At the time, Harriet was still eating things that had been birds or furry animals before they were meals, because she had not really made the connection yet, she couldn't see that shepherd's pie started out as a big friendly cow or that lamb stew was made from one of her all-time favorite animals.

Harriet cannot eat very much but my dad offers her more partly to make up for the tears situation and also because Harriet does not like a lot of food crowding up her plate at once. She might aim to have two slices of chicken breast plus a little wing and two pieces of broccoli and two crispy potato bits, but you cannot give her this straight off, you have to serve it bit by bit.

"Not touching!" Harriet nearly screams. She has been so offended tonight, she is almost fierce. How could my dad do this, especially after making her cry, how could he pass her plate back with the chicken wing touching the broccoli? I am amazed as well. I feel for Harriet. Next he makes it worse. He is a bit startled, so he just moves the food around with his finger, separating the chicken and the broccoli, and now Harriet is crying again because that is not right, you have to start all over again, put the food back, pick some different bits and lay them out properly on the plate. Shuffling it around when the pieces have already touched is no good at all.

117

Jude says, "It mixes up in your stomach. Even in your mouth it'll be touching."

"No!" wails Harriet. "Not touching! Not touching!"

It's not a good night for Harriet and I know why she likes her types of food separate on a plate; it's because up to the point when it mixes up within she can choose, she can control her world and how things go inside her. She can organize it, make it all neat and pretty before the chaos of chewing and digesting. I see her point. Also, she eats bit by bit because she is like one of the small birds she talks to and that I have read about in a book on bird life in a chapter called "The Care and Feeding of the Young Bird." Some really small birds can only take a little at a time. For instance, the pied flycatcher grown-up has to feed its baby thirty-three times an hour. Really big birds may only eat two or three times in a week and other birds, like the nighthawk, have little bills but very big mouths and they can store a lot of stuff for later inside their mouth. That is quite a good method, I think. Then there is the Eurasian swift, who will fly for hundreds of miles just to get one supper for its young who might have to wait about two days to eat. They are probably very fussy eaters and only like certain things that are hard to find. Other baby birds eat food that the grown-ups have already chewed. I am really glad Harriet is not into this way of feeding. The business of feeding chicks is pretty hard work and I read that often the parents get really tired and thin by the time the chicks are ready to sort themselves out at mealtimes without a lot of help. I read this about the mother birds, how "weight loss and mortality increased linearly with brood size." I looked up linearly. Then I numbered us all up, counting Harriet twice due to her special care and feeding needs, and came up with a brood of $5 + 1$. I thought about Mum and mortality, and this is another reason I need to watch out for Harriet. She needs special care and feeding right now, and I know I can help out. No one is going to get too thin or tired around here if I look out for Harriet, who is not crazy but more like a small chick in ways that you might not think about just by looking at her.

Just before you left me for the first time I had a dream and you were in it. This was before I pierced my hand with a knife, the little wound in my palm like the mouth of a fish feeding on the surface of a pond, opening and closing, opening and closing, and as I fainted I thought, my hand is talking to me, it is trying to tell me something. Later I thought how embarrassing my wound was, being in a classical spot for a stigmatist, even though Jesus was no doubt nailed through the wrists and not the palms at all and he was only one of many crucified types, crucifixion being a very low form of capital punishment and regularly inflicted on pirates and slaves and agitators of any kind. Constantine the Great abolished crucifixion in the fourth century, and I like him for that, I do. Before the wound, came the dream that you were in, that is, I think it was you, it seemed like you, although I hardly knew you, I still don't, fifty minutes, five times a week is never enough, but when I woke up I felt it must be you, although I cannot swear to it, or to anything at all just now, not really.

In the dream I am walking away from a building of medical arts. I don't feel well and someone passes by me and pauses and looks back, and moves on. Good, I think. I feel worse, though, and walking on, I realize my legs no longer support me. I grab a lamp-post and I am furious and ashamed at my weakness. I am determined to stay on my feet, but someone, my passerby, grips my hand firmly.

"Go away," I hiss, "I'll be okay in a minute!"

No you will not, this person conveys to me without speaking. No, not in a minute.

Now I am losing my sight and it is frightening.

"Okay!" I scream at this person. "So hold on! But don't *fucking let go!*"

"Fucking-bloody!" my sister says.

Harriet has been following me all day and copying me, doing whatever I do and daring me to get upset about it by glancing right into my face with wide-open blue eyes and her mouth all pursed up and her little chin in the air in anticipation of some kind of big reaction I just can't be bothered to give her. Mum says I should be flattered when Harriet traipses after me all over the house doing whatever I do. I don't know. Anyway, I am too tired to get upset due to the terrible wound that I have and which Harriet keeps poking at with her index finger, approaching my temple in kind of slow motion, like she is about to get poisoned by my wound or something, then touching it and pulling her hand back like she has just had an electric shock. She does this about eighteen times.

I am lying on my stomach reading a Tintin book. So is Harriet, even though she can't read French yet. Every time I turn a page, hovering near the page corner, thinking about it, she does the same. I don't care. I am recovering from my terrible wound and I am tired. Every now and again, in between pokes, Harriet says, in an amazed type voice,

"Fucking-bloody!"

This is how I got my wound. Ben, Jude and I are trying to learn something about this new country we are in and sometimes the best way is to play a typical sport, so we are doing some baseball, which is like cricket but not like cricket. For instance, the bowler does not run in toward the batsman but stands around on this little hill thinking about things and suddenly he lifts one leg and bowls at you. It's weird. Also, in cricket you can hit the ball but you do not have to run, but in baseball if you hit the ball front-ward, you have to run like crazy, and you let go of the bat too, and this strikes me as pretty typical of this new country, a kind of noisy, crazed way to play a sport.

Ben, Jude and I are playing in our bum-of-the-bag, our cul-de-sac. We do not have a bat but we did find an old iron rod down the hill at the end of our bum-of-the-bag. It was lying in a lot of scrub around the trees and bushes on the slope and we decided it would make a good baseball bat. I am the wicket-keeper, although it is called something else, I don't know what. Jude is batting and Ben is bowling, or whatever they call it in Dad's country. We don't let Harriet play but we tell her she is the umpire, just to keep her happy. She is not very good at team sports due to not having a big thing for rules written by people other than her. In our old country she was always kicking our football out of play or picking it up right in the middle of things and doing some kind of ballet with it. This would leave us speechless. She is definitely not good at team sports but you can't tell her this, I have learned, you just have to create a position for her where she can't really mess things up.

Today Harriet is the umpire. I am not sure they have one in baseball. Never mind.

It is possible I am sitting too close to the batsman, I don't know.

I remember thinking this before Jude swipes at the ball and hits me in the temple with the iron rod. That's how I got my wound, which Harriet keeps poking while saying her new favorite swear word.

"Harriet?" I say.

"Harriet?" Harriet says.

"Stop it for a minute!"

Harriet repeats this too, and I drop my head into my Tintin book and Harriet does the same.

"Harriet, didn't Dad talk to you about that word?"

"Yes! Talkies," Harriet says.

"Well? Don't you think you could just say bloody by itself, I don't know, what do you think?"

"Fuck is *not* a bad thing, Daddy said. Why can't Harriet say it? Fucking-bloody."

"Okay, Harriet."

I borrowed a book of Ben's and there was a chapter in it about the brain and it had some really good pictures and diagrams. Here is what I read. The left side and the right side of the brain have different jobs. The right = creative, the left = analytical. Right and left parts are called hemispheres. I like that, hemisphere. I copied all of this out. Left hemisphere skills = analytical thinking, digital computation, rational thinking, sequential ordering, temporal thinking, verbal skills. Right hemisphere skills = artistic ability, holistic thinking, intuition, simultaneous thinking, synthetic reasoning, visual and spatial ability. I asked Mum to explain some of these words, which is a lot easier than looking them all up. I definitely did not understand everything she said and the more I frowned the more she smiled at me. I don't think she gave me all the details. Never mind. I have enough. This is what I suspect about Harriet. All the skills in her left hemisphere, the analytical part, are also creative. Her whole brain, both hemispheres, is creative and I think that is cool, why can't everyone see that?

On the last day, before the second time you leave me, which will be for thirty-nine days and forty nights, I follow you down the hallway toward the room where we will talk for a while, and I notice how slowly you walk, this warm-weather walk that you have in almost all weathers, and I think today it is like the walk of a person who has some very bad news to tell and is not in a hurry to tell it. I also notice a stain on your left shoulder, not so much a stain as a discoloration, and I think, this is not your shirt, it belongs to a loved one and you wear it a lot probably although I have never seen it before, and I suddenly want to clasp you gently from behind and lay my right cheek just there over the stain and maybe rest there for thirty-nine days and forty nights, until I can wake up somewhere safe where I cannot hurt myself with all the deliberate energy of a crazy person.

I read that alcohol suppresses normal sleep brain waves and impairs the quality and quantity of sleep, and I don't care about this at all. Fuck it. Fucking-bloody. On the first night, I stand in the dimming light of my living room and I walk across it with my wineglass and I notice a strange blob of darkness at my feet, on the floor, and near it, two or three more dark stains. I remember the stain on your shirt, on your left shoulder, and I bend down to touch the stain and I realize it is blood. I look up at the ceiling, maybe it is coming from there. Then I see my hand, and the cut I made earlier has reopened and has been bleeding without my noticing. I hold my hand up in the air, but this is what I do first. I wash the stain out of the carpet and then I wipe the hardwood floor, I try to remove all the stains and the last thing I do is wash my wound. That is the last thing that I do.

During the summer of 1224, two years before Francis of Assisi died, he went into the mountains at La Verna to fast for forty days. He was celebrating the Assumption of the Blessed Virgin Mary and preparing for St. Michael's Day, and round about the fourteenth of September, the feast of Exaltation of the Cross, he had a vision of a beautiful crucified half-man, half-seraph with six wings. When the vision disappeared, Francis was marked with the stigmata, but he was very shy about this and was very careful thereafter to conceal the wounds. Francis was the first stigmatist, but he was reluctant, it was not his big thing, his big thing was goodness and that is so quaint, I think, so much weirder than stigmata, and now I am thinking about Harriet and how I would like to call her, but I feel too ashamed of the chaos I am making.

I do not sleep much on this night. I dream of Harriet. I watch her from the edge of a frozen night garden, brittle and starlit with shimmering snow and crystalline trees with shapes of animals carved out of the icy foliage. My sister is barefoot in a gauzy dress and she is dancing all around and she is so merry and so private I can't disturb her. I want to tell her to put some shoes on or she will catch cold. It is possible she is sleepdancing and although there is a fiction about sleepwalkers, they are not conscious and they can hurt themselves and you must watch out for them if you can. Only in REM sleep, the dream place, is the body paralyzed to prevent disaster, but in sleepwalking you are free, you are open to danger. In my dream, Harriet may be sleepdancing but she is so happy, she is okay and she has carved all these animals out of the trees. She is with all her friends and she does not need me.

. . .

I read something else in Ben's science book which is really interesting. I copy this out into a notebook because it has to do with Harriet. SYNESTHESIA/SYNESTHETICS. "These people taste words, feel flavors, and see letters in colors. Most synesthetics are women who have had synesthesia since birth. Synesthetics' brains may be structurally different, containing unusual neural pathways that carry messages to more than just one sensory cortex in the brain." The book says that you *suffer* from synesthesia but I don't think it is a bad thing at all, something you suffer from. Maybe I do not really understand it, but I think Harriet has a kind of synesthesia. I think so. Here are two examples.

We are in our old country and it is a Saturday and Harriet is five. I am eight. Harriet has been following me around all day, copying me, which is supposed to be a compliment but is driving me crazy, especially since Jude has gone off with some friends and I am in a pretty bad mood due to being left by Jude. I am sorting out some of my Action Man stuff, tidying it up and so on, even though I don't really need to, and I have it all spread out in front of me on the floor. After that I am going to read my book, *The Eagle of the Ninth* by Rosemary Sutcliff, which is really good and is about Roman soldiers, and then I will have a snack and then maybe Jude will be home. I hope so because Harriet is driving me crazy, hanging around even though I am ignoring her completely.

Harriet is playing with my little penknife which Mum bought for me in Scotland. On the hilt of the knife is a painting of Edinburgh Castle plus a whole troop of soldiers from the Black Watch in front walking up and down. I like it a lot.

"Be careful with that," I say.

"Be careful with that," Harriet repeats in a miserable voice.

I roll my eyes big time. Harriet opens up the knife, pulling out the blade, and she looks all startled when it snaps into place.

"Don't do that," I say darkly.

"Don't do that," she says, and then she throws the knife at me, just missing my left ear. Wow. Wow. Look what she did. Harriet's eyes are real spooked now and there is a silence between us as we sit cross-legged on the floor, face to face.

Mum passes by our room and she looks in and Harriet swivels her little body toward Mum and she starts wailing right away, that's what she does, and she says,

"Jem threw the knife! Jem threw the knife at Harriet!"

I am eleven now and when I read Ben's book, I remember this knife-throwing act and I know this is synesthesia. Harriet was not lying, it is just how she saw things, that I was throwing a knife at her, all Saturday morning, because I was not looking out for her that day when she wanted me to.

Example number two. It is night and Harriet is eight. We are asleep but Harriet wakes me up. She rises up from her bed and her little white nightdress glows in the dark. She is very straight up, all the vertebrae piled properly and so on, then she leaps up into the windowsill, which is quite a bit smaller than the one in the old bedroom we shared in our old country, and she flaps her feather-weight arms and bats them lightly against the windowpanes. Now I am worried and I am aware of my heart thumping and I climb onto the sill but I try not to show I am worried she will fall right out of the window so I push it closed slowly and take hold of her ankle in the softest grip I can manage.

"Harriet?"

"Yes," she says in a strange voice, kind of anxious and loud.

"What are you doing?"

"Going outside," she says, much more awake now, because she sounds like Harriet again and the tears are coming. "I'm flying," she says. "Playing with the birds. Fly. Fly."

"Shall we do a card game, Harriet? Do you want to?" That's what we usually do when Harriet sleepwalks or just can't sleep, we play card games she never knows the rules to, or we make bird shadows on the wall, birds that go "gloo-gloo, gloo-gloo" for some reason I can't remember just now, or else I sing to her, quite badly, but she likes it anyway.

"Sing," says Harriet.

Okay, baby. Okay.

That is example number two. Harriet feels like a bird. So Harriet can fly.

"Is it a man or a woman?" my friend asks me in a parked car in my street, also a cul-de-sac, a bum-of-the-bag, where I live now, grown up and on my own. I just want to go home. I hate questions and I feel like Harriet who rarely had time for questions, not seeing the point of them at all and never really answering them in the way most people expect you to, with some kind of immediacy and logic, most of all, logic.

At the first convent where Harriet and I both went, there was once a changeover of order, and gray nuns we knew so well became blue nuns we did not know at all, and with them came new rules, such as the option of bringing your own lunch. This was the very best bit about the new order and Mum packed lunches for us that were full of marvels, including little notes written in her elegant script that always sloped diagonally across a page with maybe, "Hello, little goose!" or "See you soon, darling," and these notes would be tucked in amongst leftover dinner-party food, smoked salmon, deviled eggs, lovely things that other kids gathered round us to stare at.

Today Harriet has lost her lunch and I do not ask her anything about it because she will not answer me. She looks hungry and she tugs at my sleeve and I let her scoot in next to me, even though she is not supposed to sit at my table, she should be at the table with the little kids. Never mind.

Sister Lucille says, "Harriet, where is your lunch?" She doesn't ask very patiently. She is not curious, she is cross.

Harriet squeezes in closer to me, burying her chin in her chest but twisting around a little to glance at me from the corner of her eye.

"She—" I start to answer for Harriet.

"Jemima Weiss! I asked your sister!"

Bloody.

"The badger went in the hole. Little badgers inside!" says Harriet without looking at Sister Lucille. Harriet is going to start crying any second, I can feel her body shivering. I wish Sister Lucille would go away and I think how Mum would guess right off what happened, how she would understand that Harriet was playing in an out-of-bounds area in the playground, that she had gone astray without being quite lost and had found some animals, a badger going into his house, and she had left her lunch for the badger and his family. It's not hard to see this. You can easily upset Harriet with questions and it is best to avoid them unless you understand

Harriet the way I do and do not think she is crazy, which she is not, no.

"Is it a man or a woman?"

"A woman." Who cares. Leave me alone.

"Is it working for you?"

Fuck off. "I don't know. Yes, I mean. Maybe."

"What is her name?"

Why are you asking me this. "I am not going to tell you," I say quietly.

"Fine," my friend says, glancing at me the way you do at a dangerous person, a deranged person.

I won't share you, I can't share you because right now I can't tell the difference between sharing and outright loss and I might lose you, someone might take you away from me before I even know who you are and why I need you. I think of Harriet and how she went into the world out of my sight, to be shared, I guess, and she went places where I couldn't look out for her and I lost it, my special job of looking out for her. I want it back.

When Harriet wakes up in the morning, her hair flying all around, she is happy because she realizes breakfast is coming up pretty soon and breakfast is her favorite meal. Saturday is Harriet's favorite day because after the breakfast thought she has another big happy jolt and that has to do with not having to haul on a lot of clothes she does not feel like wearing, like gloves and a hat, a tie, tunic, pullover, stripy pinafore and the right color socks depending on the season, which is another complication for Harriet, a different uniform according to the season. On a sunny winter morning Harriet wants to wear white gloves and a straw hat but she is not allowed, it's in the rules. Also, she has to wear a hat on the way to school or you can get reported and some days she hates this.

"No hat! Can't see the sky! Stop it! Get off!"

When it is really bad with Harriet, I hold the hat and hover near her, ready to clap it right onto her head when we get too close to school.

Often when I let go of Harriet and shove her gently toward the little kids' entrance in the courtyard, she turns around and gives me a painful look, like maybe I have made a big mistake and she should stay with me, go where I go, because really bad things are going to happen to her now, but I have to leave her, it's what I have to do.

"See you tomorrow," she says.

"Right here at the gates, Harriet."

"Okay."

Harriet knows we meet at ten to four P.M., she knows it, but it is so long until she is free again that it will feel like tomorrow, and that is another thing about Harriet, that it is whatever time she feels, which can be a pretty good way to be, having your own way with time, especially on Saturdays for instance. On Saturday she feels so happy, all she will eat that day is breakfast, like she is waking up on a Saturday, all day long. Even at supper, Harriet will have Baby Familia, her favorite cereal, a Swiss muesli type cereal that comes in very tiny bits with dusted raisins. This is what she will eat when we are all having something like shepherd's pie or fish or sausages with mashed potatoes. It's cool and nobody minds at all.

.　　.　　.

Do you think it's cruel that in the hour you have for me there are only fifty minutes? When you say, rather softly, "Well," and then you pause and you add, "it's time," and then you stand up, watching me in my crazed flurry of leave-taking, that awful moment, do you mean, "I am sorry, it's not me, it's time," like telling me to fuck off out of here is not your fault at all, sending me out into the world where I came from, where up to the first minute and from the fifty-first minute, all my hours contain sixty whole minutes, some endless and others frighteningly brief? Or do you just mean to remind me with these three words, "Well, it's time," that this is one way I can measure my life, just one way to do it?

One day I think you should take me home and let me sit at your table, a stranger there, to watch you with your family and learn stuff. I think you should. I know one thing though, I know that a family can start with one fantasy you have nothing to do with and end in another, your own, and the problem is the space between, and maybe you do take me home, for a little bit every day, making me take a look at things I don't want to see, like Harriet sick, near dying and me not there, me not there at all.

I was not there because we were not Harriet and Jem, we were strangers, and the distance between her country and mine was the least of it and so I could not really know how bad it was with her, how she lay nearly lifeless, so unlike Harriet, with tubes going in and out and a lot of poison flooding her body and a great wound in her side. Peritonitis, they said, one of the worst cases they had ever seen. Maybe the tubes were the worst thing because when Mum told me how Harriet tried to shrug them off, pull them out,

Mum seeing in this Harriet's first signs of return to life, I thought about Jude's red cardinals. Jude had a lot of birds once, doves, finches, canaries and then he saved and saved and bought a red cardinal and mostly he let them fly all about in one room which we converted for the birds, and only at night, when he could not be watching out for them, he'd lock them in their cages. He found his red cardinal dead three days after he bought it, his neck all twisted, and he bought one more and the same thing happened. Then he was told by someone who knew about birds that cardinals cannot be caged. They can't stand it and they will die, which is exactly what happened.

I keep thinking about Harriet's awful wound and I have this particular idea, which may be a crazy one, it's possible. This is it. Even though Harriet is healed now, I want to put my hands in her wound, in her side, I want to put my hands inside and wash them there and then maybe I will be okay for all time. I see it very clearly, this hand-washing inside Harriet.

"Why do you wear that?" you ask, indicating the bracelet I have fashioned out of surgical bandaging, cutting a piece to size and stapling it together to fit my wrist, with, as you pointed out to me, the scratchy ends of the staples against my skin.

Haircloth/hairshirt, worn by religious penitents, becoming a popular upholstery material in the nineteenth century.

"People might see the cuts and think I am crazy," I said.

"Oh. I thought maybe *you* do not want to see."

I think Francis of Assisi had a sense of humor. He saw all things as a reflection of God, the elements, people, disasters, illness, parts of the body, all things. He called everyone and everything Brother this and Sister that, and he even gave his illnesses nicknames, apologizing to "Brother Ass the Body" for all the pain it had to endure, including a horrible eye disease near the end of his life. He definitely had a sense of humor. You might not have had a fine dinner in his hut, due to his big thing for austerity, but you would have been entertained, I think so.

Tonight I walk all around my flat, and I talk aloud. I look at the knife that cut me.

"Brother Knife!" I say.

I see my blood. "Sister Blood, hello!"

"Brother Pasta Sauce, Sister Telephone, Brother Books, Brother Mirror, Sister Soap!"

I am laughing now. Is this crazy or what?

"Sister Crazy!" I announce. "Sister Crazy."

Now we are Harriet and Jem again, her scar is nearly nine years old and I think maybe I have synesthesia too, when it comes to Harriet, that is, because sometime, I don't know when, I looked at Harriet and she became my big sister and she looked back at me and I am the baby sister and it is like when we were little kids and her big thing for chocolate became my big thing and my big thing for cheese became hers but only on birthdays, in a cake situation.

For a few days during your break, I am in Harriet's house, which is gracious, inviting, elegant, and has peculiarities such as this. You open a door and across the room, at a point your eye is naturally drawn to, is a stuffed animal sitting on a radiator or in a windowsill or somewhere, a lamb or a mouse, a dog, a bear, and it makes you smile, it really does. My sister draws animals for a living. She paints in her own time, working all night or just for a morning, in her own house, a place she made, a space she knows.

I am in the spare bedroom and Harriet comes in with her dog who gets in bed with me and starts licking my wrists. The dog, Harriet says, knows when you are upset and licks and licks until you rise up out of it. It has to be true because usually this dog ignores me completely, knowing, I guess, that I do not have a big thing for pets.

"Harriet?"

Harriet sits on the bed and looks right at me.

"Harriet. Sometimes—do you ever get—you know—a big urge to just get up and pack a small bag and go home but you don't know where that is anymore, you don't know which way to go?"

And Harriet does not answer, not with immediacy and logic, anyway, but she tells me all the things she made for lunch, the pea soup that has been cooking in fresh stock for days and that she will serve in white bowls with carved lion heads on the sides; the pissaladière she will lay on colorful plates with hand-painted birds on them, keeping aside my favorite plate for me, the one with the blood-red bird like a cardinal. As she tells me this she strokes away a wisp of my hair which is wet because I am crying like an idiot, like a crazy person, and my hair is tangling up in my eyelashes. She does this really gently.

Crazy is not a person, it is a place you go, it is the maze inside Harriet without Harriet to guide you, it is standing in the eye of a storm with all the windows open, because you think you ought to take it, something Harriet always knew not to do. Please let me out of here. Please come back.

Harriet has a big thing for animals but she knows the difference between an animal and a person. She is not crazy. Harriet gets up off the bed and she walks out of my room and her dog follows.

PERILOUS BOY

I hardly ever drink spirits but when I do, I like this single malt
called Bowmore, and I keep a bottle of the twelve year old in the
place where I live. It is considered the flag-bearer of the Bowmore
range. I like this word flag-bearer, it makes me think of nine-
teenth-century warfare when usually the youngest and fairest boys
would be selected to carry the flag and bang the drum ahead of
the troops, and they represented the spirit of the army and would
feel great pride in their task of flag-bearing and drumbeating and
the uniform they wore was probably the finest suit of clothes they
had ever slipped into and maybe leading the troops into battle
was the most glamorous moment in their lives and the fact they

were likely to die first, in some really gruesome way, walking targets, did not concern them much because they were flag-bearers, and this is a very glorious thing to be. At the end of a battle, if your flag-bearer was still alive, you would consider yourself a very lucky soldier, truly blessed. When you do a really dangerous thing, it's good to have some kind of symbol you can recognize to keep you going. It's a little bit like the Holy Grail business. All those perilous journeys through maybe a sea of dragons and tussles with death and black-clad women and so on were not about winning some old cup which would be not a lot different from any old cup lying around a knight's own house. No. It was just a reminder that you are actually aiming for something, not just tussling with death for no particular reason, like going for a walk at night with no destination but leaving a light on in your house so no one thinks you are some kind of crazy person out on the loose. The light shows you have a purpose, an end point, and you know what you are doing and where you are going, even if you don't at all, not in the least.

I take it out sometimes, this bottle of Bowmore, and I admire it, the way it has no label but the information is silk-screened right onto the bottle, this flag-bearing bottle. This is what it says. "BOWMORE, ISLAY, single malt Scotch whisky years 12 old, 70cle, 40% vol. Distilled and bottled in Scotland." The e mark next to 70cl indicates the contents are guaranteed within the European Community and cannot be challenged. There is also a little oval portrait right under the shoulders of the bottle, depicting a part of Islay, which is the most southerly of the Hebrides. It shows a lot of white gulls flying over some blue sea and in the distance there are buildings with red rooftops. I think this is the distillery itself, which overlooks Loch Laggan, and at the edges of the oval picture are these words: "Estab" and "1779" and at the bottom is the word "Islay." It's a pretty bottle, it really is.

Sometimes I pull out the cork and I smell the malt, I nose it, as they say. The man in charge at Bowmore is a bit romantic, I think, but not soppy. He started as a cooper when he was only fifteen years old and he describes the maturing whisky in the casks as growing really intense and concentrated, with the angels' share working away quietly the way it does. This man says you can only control part of the process when making single malt, that much of it is out of your hands once the maturing is under way, and he compares this to bringing up a healthy kid in a good home, that there is only so much you can do for a while and then you push it out into the world and your job is more or less over. He adds that now the malt is in the hands of Time, like the kid, and he uses a capital letter for Time, which is where he gets a bit soppy. Never mind.

Here is the real reason I keep this bottle in the place where I live. It is for my dad. In fact I have not had one single sip from it, not a dram as they are supposed to say in Scotland. This bottle is for him, in case he drops by, but although I do not live very far from him, he never comes. It's okay though, because he might, and it would be bad news if I did not have any single malt to offer him when he does. Then I'll pull it out of the cupboard real casual like I have a whole lot of single malt whisky bottles lurking in there and I pull them out all the time, not just for him. I won't make a fuss in any way. We'll be like cowboys at a bar in a western.

Something else about Bowmore I really like. Bowmore is the capital of Islay and in it, at the top of a sloping street, is a round church that was built in 1767. It was built round so that there would be no place for the devil to hide. Cool.

· · ·

"Jude?"

I start my countdown. I have to do it aloud because Jude has his eyes closed. Usually I just hold out my two fists in front of me and unfurl my fingers one by one and I have a concentrated look on my face. Jude knows exactly what I am doing, which is counting down the seconds between asking him something and getting an answer. I am beginning to think this countdown thing is not useful at all and that Jude enjoys it and that Jude maybe takes even longer to answer me than anyone else. Jude and I are real close. For instance, if I am having a snack and Jude is strolling by, he will take it right out of my hands and eat a bite, making a really neat bite shape so you can count each one of his teeth, and then he will pass it back to me quite slowly.

When I was a little kid, I would come home from my school, my first convent, and shuck off my uniform as soon as possible and haul on some jeans and also some old top of Jude's. I loved to wear his clothes, especially this navy-blue rugby jersey he had which was all wool and had an open V-neck with a proper collar like on a regular shirt. I also liked his old school vests in summertime, white ones without sleeves which made me feel like a World War II soldier on a day off, in a state of undress when he would get busy polishing up his uniform or having beer with other soldiers and discussing commando raids or something. I was living through a stage of tucking my hair in my collar, even at school, because it felt like short boy hair, just like Jude's, instead of long and unruly and girly like my own or Harriet's, which was even girlier, flying all around in a fluffy manner like angels on Christmas cards.

When I became girly in ways harder and harder to hide, things got a little tense, and I had the feeling for a while that Jude thought I had betrayed him or something. It was just a stage with Jude and he never said much about it as usual, but it made him cross until he got used to things and how we had to make adjustments the way you do. I remember one hot Saturday when we were lurking in the garden with Ben, a bit slaphappy due to heat and having no homework to do, and Jude pulled off his shirt and flung it on the grass.

"Hot," he said, glancing around at us. Ben does not like to take his shirt off, he seems to have a different temperature situation going on with him, or maybe it is this gothic thing, what he calls the gothic imagination, which involves staying swaddled all the time and not exposing flesh to daylight like the vampires and other beasts he likes to read about, I don't know, but nobody expects Ben to fling his shirt off today.

"Hot," I said. A trickle of water ran down my neck. It's not a bad feeling.

"Take your top off then," Jude snapped.

"I can't."

"Why not!" Jude said, and I could see the blue veins pulsing at his temples, the ones with all the offshoots I call his train tracks because that's what they look like, railroad tracks.

"Shut up!" I told Jude and I stormed off into the house.

This was only a phase with Jude and I don't think he understood it at all. He probably won't remember if I tell him about it now, which I won't, as he doesn't like that kind of thing.

". . . eleven, twelve, thirteen. Jude? JUDE!"

"Mmmm?" goes Jude, opening up his blue eyes just for a second and swiveling them in my direction without moving his head.

Mmmm, meaning, what is the fuss all about, why do we have to do any speaking at all. Then he closes his eyes up again. This is why. (1) It is a pretty hot bright day and he is lying on his back on the dock at our summer cottage and he is facing into the sun and his eyes are very sensitive, just like mine in fact, maybe just because we have cold-climate blue eyes. (2) Jude is reading, something he likes to do with his eyes shut and the book open on his chest. It happens this way: the words are absorbed into his bloodstream and travel on up to his brain. I know this to be true because I often pick his book up and he is usually at the same spot, for instance, the fence-painting part in *The Adventures of Tom Sawyer*, which is a book my dad gives him to read every summer when Jude never says, you gave me that book already. He just walks away with it, nodding, and every summer he leaves the book face down somewhere at the fence-painting part, but, this is the cool thing, he knows the whole story. He can recite bits of dialogue. I know he has read the book in his special way because I tried to read *The Adventures of Tom Sawyer* just to see why my dad feels so strongly about giving it to Jude every year, and I can never get past the fence-painting part and I slammed the book down once and then Jude looked over at me and slowly told me all the good bits and also the boring bits. That's how I figured out his reading method and do not worry about it, unlike my dad, who shouts at Jude about not reading enough and leaving books open face down, creasing up the spine, something my dad hates.

"Jude! Is that your book?" my dad will say, pointing angrily at some face-down book, usually *The Adventures of Tom Sawyer*. "What did I tell you?"

I worry about my dad when he gets angry, I feel a bit sorry for him because it is such a big noisy thing with him, and so ferocious and he comes even more undone than he normally is, his hair flopping in curls over his forehead which is all furrowed like that hard part of the beach where the sea has been rushing in and out over it, and you want to tell him, it's okay, Dad, it's just a book, or make him sit down and take some deep breaths or something. Also, he seems the most ruffled of all, none of his kids paying him that much attention or getting spooked but just taking it in, this outburst, like when a door slams shut suddenly and you just want to know which door it is, and you look at the door like it could explain to you why it just did that, slamming shut out of nowhere.

Jude is the least ruffled of all. "Don't leave books open face down," he says, real calm and polite but a bit bored.

"RIGHT!" shouts my dad.

Then Jude will reach over slowly, very slowly, and rearrange the book, closing it up and laying it on one side the way Dad likes, but forgetting to slip in a bookmark due to never ever remembering a bookmark, which is why he leaves books face down in the first place, having better things to do than traipse all over the house looking for one, like today, lying on his back in the sun on the dock with me, reading with his eyes closed under a hot blue sky.

"What are you reading?"

Jude levers the book about four centimeters off his chest, like this is hard work. He means, you know what I'm reading, you can see.

"Haven't you read that about eight times?" I say.

"Is that what you wanted to ask me?"

"No."

"What then," says Jude, not sounding all that curious.

It does not mean he is not curious. It's a thing with him, like he is right there with you but not there at all, in some other place always, at the very same time as being with you. You have to accept this with Jude and when he can relax and be this way with you, there and not there, you know he likes being around you. If you find it weird, though, and need his immediate attention, like answers to questions, little movements, looks in the eyes and so on, he will not stick around long, he'll walk away because it makes him very tired and cross having to talk straight off or move his body a lot. Most of the time he is just searching for things, a bit like a medieval knight on a quest, which is something I am reading about right now.

"Do you know what Ben is doing at night?" I say this quietly, in a voice meaning I am about to make a revelation to Jude on the subject of Ben.

"What." Jude still has closed-up eyes.

"He keeps beers in the cupboard behind his clothes cupboard, you know, the crawl space with spiders and junk and stuff. He takes the screen out of the bedroom window, climbs off the roof, and he comes right down here and pushes out in the boat and drinks beers in the middle of the lake or somewhere."

"Yeh."

"Yeh—what?"

"He picks up Kate first," says Jude.

"Kate? Kate?" I am a bit startled now and get the same foolish feeling as when I showed Harriet a private place I like to hide out in in the woods on the hill going down to the lake, revealing it like I was letting her in on some big secret, and she just looked at me all fluffy-haired and smiley and dug up her treasure tin which she had buried right in the same place. This contained pieces of chocolate and chocolate-covered biscuits and she offered me a piece of anything I wanted. She had been coming here for ages, just not at the same time as I did, and she probably followed me here once, hopping around in the trees like some kind of fairy. It was nice of Harriet to offer up some chocolate, for which she has a really big thing, but still, I felt sort of cheated and a bit grumpy like right now with Jude, who is not at all surprised by what I told him.

"Rich girl yacht club Kate, where Ben works? The place with the tennis court?"

"Yup."

"He goes out with her?"

Jude does not answer and I cannot picture this date situation, this pairing of Ben with Kate. "Ben and Kate. Weird. You know her dad keeps lecturing Ben about every little bit of work he does? You know, here's how to hold a broom, here's how to swish it across the floor. Here's how to mow, here's how to bang a hammer. Bloody. I bet he shows him how to eat lunch. Here's how to bite a sandwich, approach it slowly, start at the corner, bla-bla . . . So he just sits out in the bay with Kate and a pile of beers?"

"He's too noisy coming back in," says Jude. "I told him to just go out the front door. That's what I do anyway."

"You go out on the lake at night with beers?"

"And it's better to tie the beers to the dock and hang them in the water. That way they're cold by night."

"Right," I say. I look at Jude with the book open on his chest, his chest which is hairy, unlike Ben's which is hairless, due to his vampire blood probably, I look at Jude with his eyes shut in the sun and I wonder for maybe the first time about all the things I do not know about my brother who is nearly my twin and is lying right next to me with his eyes closed, and I have this big feeling in me like when a car stops but you are still moving forward and there is a prickly rush of sensation in your stomach and the big feeling has to do with wanting to be with Jude and go where he goes, always. I would not be a drag, I would not talk much and I could look after myself, but I could just be with him and we'd go places together, like knights, like Perceval and Galahad for instance.

"Can I come one night?"

"May I," Jude says, imitating Mum's voice, gentle and sort of airy, like she is not actually correcting you.

"Yeh-yeh. Will you take me?"

"No," says Jude. "You wouldn't like it. I go with Joe."

"Joe's okay."

"No," says Jude. "It's rough."

"Farty burpy bad joke rough?"

"Yuh." Jude pauses for a while and I look up the hill because I can see Gus in the corner of my eye. Here he comes with his fishing rod. Gus is really intense this summer and seems to have only two activities. (1) Eating tinned tomato soup for breakfast, real slow and precise, tipping the bowl away from him and scooping up shallow spoonfuls from the surface, and (2) Fishing. I hope he is not about to fish off the dock. I hate that because it puts me right off swimming as all I can think about is fishies with pulsing gills and slimy bodies and wriggly worms on the end of hooks. Gus has the longest legs on a small boy I have ever seen and he is really graceful and makes me think of the colts at the farm near our place. Gus has asthma this year but he pretends he doesn't. He fights it like a knight and we all look out for him, listening hard for that tinny rasp that signals danger for Gus.

Jude says, "I'll take you out for a beer in town."

"When?"

"Next time."

"Cool." I don't press Jude for details. He doesn't like that, it makes him anxious and cross. He'll take me. He won't forget.

Gus is definitely coming this way.

"Gus, why do you have to fish here?"

Gus just looks at me and is clearly not even thinking about fishing anyplace else.

"Do *not* put that tin of wrigglies anywhere near me, Gus." I say this in quite a threatening way and this is what Gus does. He does his imitation of a water snake he once saw skimming over the lake toward him when he was fishing in the brook, standing in the water in huge Wellington boots. It is pretty funny when he does it and sometimes I ask him to do it for me when I need to laugh. He widens his eyes a little bit, looking a bit spooked but very serious and he darts his tongue in and out at odd intervals. It creases me up right now and it's kind of hard to stay mad at him. It's hard not to laugh. That's how it is.

"Well, you better not be casting around here, that's all I have to say. I'm not getting a hook in my eye, okay? Gus! I'm talking to you!"

"I'll be careful," he says.

"Oh God. I'm going up to the house."

Jude does not move but he says, "Stay."

Okay. I lie back and I rest my head on Jude's stomach, warning him first so he doesn't throw me off, and I also tell him not to do the trampoline, which involves flexing his belly so my head jumps all around and I get whiplash. I hate lying straight on the dock though because my head gets all bruisy. I look up at the sky. I keep an eye on Gus who is casting. I think about my brothers and how they are solid, not shifty or nervous but solid, like sculptures.

You can walk around them and they'll just take you in and when they move away, you can still feel the space they filled, like they have carved out a place in the atmosphere, and if you follow in their footsteps, I think, you will be walking a straight and determined line with no messing about, no crazy veering off in all directions, and each step will have the same weight, the same impression on the earth or snow or whatever surface they are making their way over. I think Harriet and Mum and me are not like this, we are different, and maybe that's okay, I don't know yet.

The sun is strong and I close my eyes. Just like Jude. I'll have to trust Gus, that's all.

When the summer is over, which is not yet, not for another thirty-seven long days in fact, I will be going back to school and it will be my fourth year at my second convent, which is full of Italian nuns who are a little bit noisy and speak Italian to each other and French to us, the girls. Sometimes they speak Italian right next to you and look at you at the same time and I call this dodgy behavior, maybe not even Christian. You know they are talking about you, sometimes with spooky smiles on their faces and once, a pair of them, one tall, one short, were doing this, having a fishy little chat about me, when the tall one peeled off down the corridor, throwing her head back and cackling like she had just heard the funniest thing on earth, leaving the short one looking at me with a wily expression. Kind of satisfied. There is not a lot you can do at times like this and you have to face the facts. One thing though. It made me nostalgic for Irish nuns at my old convent, in my old country where I was born, because they did not give a kid a headache and were not spooky at all.

Soeur Rosa is the religion-Latin-art nun. She is a big reader and does not sleep much, worrying a lot, I guess, about humanity and the problem of sin, especially where it concerns her favorite girls, ones she calls her *beautées fatales*. Fatal beauties. Two other things. Soeur Rosa is allergic to peanuts. Soeur Rosa resembles Mussolini. I can never tell her this last thing of course, but I can't help thinking it. I have seen a few pictures of this man, although I always speed right on by the one with him hanging upside down from a lamppost, and the similarity is there, it just is. Occasionally I have an urge to point this out to her, like on the day she tells me my father has the eyes of a wild animal in the jungle. This was really weird. What was I supposed to say to that? She has seen him pick me up once, as we were going shopping or something after school plus she has seen his photo in the newspaper I was reading, the photo they use on his sports column. When she said the word wild, which is *sauvage* in French, she made her eyes go all wide open and stary. I decided her bad feeling about my dad was a veiled warning to me due to my dad being Jewish, which is not a religion the nuns recommend. They believe their own is tops and they are pretty keen for you to know it and can be a bit touchy if you don't have a lot of time for faith. This is something else I have learned, how easy it is to freak them out on the subject of God or *le Seigneur* as they like to call him.

Here is when I decided it was a good idea to spook Soeur Rosa on the subject of *le Seigneur*, her big cheese, the one to whom she is married, like all the other nuns, and for whom she has renounced worldly things, which to me is a big mistake. Let's face it. She got it wrong. I have learned quite a lot about this due to my private study of medieval knights on the big quest and to conversations with my brother Ben, who has a big thing for alchemy. For instance, when Perceval finished up all his adventures and sorted out the sick Grail King in the Castle, I think it must have gone to his head because here is where he slips up. Instead of bashing off back to King Arthur and taking up the empty place at the Round Table, the dangerous seat, *le siège périlleux*, the one only the best and most virtuous knight can sit in without any mishaps occurring like the seat splitting or thunderclaps rending things in two and all kinds of mayhem, instead of doing this and bringing harmony back from the Grail Castle, he has a fit of holiness and renounces worldly things. And that was a pity, it really was, because there was devastation again and the Round Table split up and Mordred came along and there were a lot of weeping knights, and dead ones too, and even Arthur had to retire and Merlin went mad. It was a bad state of affairs altogether and should have been a warning to people who opt for holiness and stick with other holy types. I don't think there is much point in my telling Soeur Rosa all this. I don't think so. The nuns have got it wrong but you cannot tell them, it would be too hard on them.

Here is what happens. I am running late and I race up the cloakroom steps, my shoelaces flapping and my arms full of books I have no time to sift through, deciding I'll probably need them all anyway, and of course I trip up the steps, which is one of the topmost annoying ways of tripping except for hitting an uneven paving stone on the sidewalk when you are walking along all cool and lofty and suddenly you are leaping into the void limbs akimbo and you feel like an idiot.

My books fly up into the air and my homework book, a heavy little hard-backed volume issued to you by the convent and onto which I have plastered cutout photos of heroes, such as Peter Gabriel, David Bowie, Alan Ladd as Shane, Marlon Brando and that sports-column shot of my dad depicting his savage look, this book of mine lands right at Soeur Rosa's feet. She is at her usual lookout post, glaring out through the large picture window at convent girls approaching school from their homes with various expressions of gloom and dread on their faces, some of them taking a last defiant haul on a Gitane.

"Jesus Christ!" I exclaim, retrieving my books.

"Mlle Weiss?" says Soeur Rosa, folding her stubby Mussolini forearms, revealing some flesh, always a shock, like seeing a wisp of hair escape from the wimple. She has one eyebrow lifted and a sly Italian grin is starting up on her face, making my heart sink.

"Aren't you Jewish, Mlle Weiss?"

If I had a glove, I'd slap it right down on the tiled floor between us, I am in the mood for a duel, I really am, but maybe a swift chop from a broadsword would be more satisfying, I don't know. I don't answer her. She is not expecting me to.

"You do not believe in Jesus Christ," she says.

"He was a fine teacher," I say, which is what I've heard from Mum and it seems to wrap things up pretty neatly and is also guaranteed to exasperate a nun. Soeur Rosa gives me a pitying look though, as if to say, oh dear, oh dear, jungle child, you have so much to learn. Then she adds,

"You know the Jews murdered Jesus Christ, you understand this?" she announces, checking me out for a guilty look.

Bloody. Not that murder rap business again and suddenly Soeur Rosa is not Mussolini, she is a great detective, a vain but brainy type, Hercule Poirot maybe, and she is strolling up and down a closed drawing room where a lot of Jews are sitting bolt upright on uncomfortable chairs, fidgeting with cups of lemon tea and looking downright shifty and Soeur Rosa is asking them where they were at the time of death and so on, and without eye-ing him directly, out of nowhere, she hauls out a yarmulke from her pocket, one with a bloodstain on it.

"Peter? I believe you are missing your hat?"

I am quite keen to bring up the Inquisition but I don't. First of all, I am tired and annoyed this morning and Soeur Rosa is breath-ing across at me with garlic and espresso breath and also, I am too polite. Next time though, I will be better armed. I am going to talk to Ben and listen hard.

I am in Ben's room in our city house and there is a thing about Ben's room, whatever place we are living in, that it is always dark. He usually gets to pick a room first whenever we move into a place, due to being the oldest, and maybe he just chooses a room on the dark side. Then I think about the other rooms on the same side of the house and they are not all that dark, not really, so maybe it's Ben, which gives me an odd feeling but not a bad one. I believe Ben is one with the dark side, not the kind of dark that makes you cross, stumbling around and stubbing your toe cross, but a kind of dark that is like light almost. I also think about this business of the oldest getting to choose first and I decide this is okay because when you are the oldest you have a lot more responsibilities and this can make you tired and pretty sensitive and therefore you need to be in a room that is right for you, and so none of us mind this. Ben does a lot for us and he is very sensitive and there is a pile of work to do such as this afternoon, giving me an alchemy lesson so I can fox Soeur Rosa and get her to stop accusing me of murder.

Ben is sitting on his bed cross-legged and he is surrounded by books. I am on the floor because Ben might need to stretch out and his legs are so long there will definitely be no room for me to sit up there with him. I cross my legs too. I am ready.

"First of all," he says. "The Eucharist. Transubstantiation. In a way, what your nuns are doing is a bit primitive."

"Whoa," I say. I like that.

"They are still stuck in a concrete view of things. This is blood, this is flesh and so on, but in the ninth century, Erigena——"

"How do you spell that?"

"Just a minute," says Ben, not cross but pretty serious.

"Sorry, Ben."

"No problem. Erigena was into a more mystical type of thing and what he said was the Sacrament was a symbolic thing and it had a spiritual effect on your feelings and he was considered a heretic for this, but what he was onto was a kind of higher level of spirituality, of consciousness and so on, you see? It's all symbols."

Relax, I could say to Soeur Rosa. Cool your jets, it's just a symbol.

"Right," I say.

"It's a lot like the Grail business—how are you doing with that Grail book I gave you?"

"Nearly finished. It's great."

"Okay. Well, the Grail is like going for this higher state, the self archetype——"

"Archetype?"

"Yeh. It's the big thing, you know, like a model, a sort of symbol of symbols, right? The big thing. Power."

"The big thing," I repeat.

"Yup. So the self is also a Christ-image, you see, and Perceval goes for it and in alchemy it's there too, it's about wholeness, the whole guy with good and evil, consciousness and the unconscious all in one. It's called the union of the opposites. That's what Perceval could have achieved if he sat in the *siège périlleux,* which is supposed to be the seat Judas left when he betrayed Christ at the Last Supper, you see, and that's another reason the Grail in alchemy is also a stone—"

"Wait," I say, slapping my hands over my eyes, like now there is too much light in Ben's room, of the dark kind of course. "The Grail is also a stone?"

"Jem, you have to let go of this cup idea, okay? It's the same thing, an image of whole psychic man, but the alchemists were interested in spirit in reality, in, you know, material stuff, less remote than Christian thought, and for medieval poets like Chrétien and so on, they were more kind of emotional and the vessel or cup is a more feminine image."

"More feminine?"

"Yup. It's like a person is a vessel for the unconscious. Here, listen. 'The vessel becomes a uterus for the spiritual renewal of the individual.' "

"Yuk."

"This is good too. When God was having strife with Satan, the Grail stone is left on Earth and the angels who didn't take sides, sort of doubting angels, ones who believed in the balance of things, the unity of opposites and so on, they guard the stone. See?"

"I guess," I say, a bit weakly.

"Just remember. It's a light-dark thing and Christianity kind of leaves this behind, okay?"

"Yeh," I say.

Ben stretches out and a couple of books fall on the floor. He leaves it that way and leans on his side, raising up on an elbow. He says, kind of perky now, sensing confusion, "You know about the Fourth man?"

What's up? Are we on something new? Cold War, spies? Probably not. It's safest to say no, which is what I do. "No."

"The nuns will hate this, Jem. Lucifer. Satanael. The devil is the Fourth man. The Antichrist. Nuns only get the light side like with transubstantiation, right? They don't see the death part at all, the blood, the vessel as a grave and the devil as a divine reality too, the invisible opponent, the other son of God who makes up a Quaternity which is more whole than a Trinity thing, and it's everywhere in the Grail stuff but they kind of sneak right past it in Christian thought. Merlin has the light and dark side of Christ. He is Duplex. Like Mercurius in alchemy—"

"Mercurius?"

"Forget Mercurius for now. Forget about it. Merlin is a bit like the Grail because of inner wholeness of the self but also he has a kind of demon within, which means he can use nature to serve man, like a scientist, which is what alchemists were, before real science. But Merlin loses his mind sort of and withdraws from the world. Maybe it was all too much for him."

"Like Perceval." I am getting a headache.

"Yeh."

"And Merlin goes to live in the forest with his sister," I add, not sure what I want to say but keen to show I am still with Ben, still listening hard.

"That's right. The brother-sister archetype."

"Really?"

"Yes," says Ben with authority, picking a book off the floor. "Here. 'A figure embodying the dual aspect of the arcane substance.' "

"What's that?"

"Um. It's an archetype thing and a blood thing. The arcane

substance is blood. So the stone has a soul, right? And Dorn said, 'in the final operations,' the stone releases an *obscurus* type liquid, blood you know, and this is a prophecy of a redeemer who will bleed and be healing and so on. Okay?" Ben says, tired now, racing to a finish.

"What final operations?"

"Not sure. I'm working on it."

"Cool. Thanks, Ben."

I lie back on the floor and cross my legs at the ankles, resting them up on the edge of Ben's bed, and I fold my arms behind my head like Ben but my fingers get all mashed due to the hard floor so I lay them on my stomach, with the uterus vessel underneath there somewhere, and I think about Ben and how much he knows, all the books he has read and how he is a good teacher, always patient and making things interesting, even difficult things. I think that maybe he should not have to mess with school because he is not good at most of the things they teach him there and it takes up a lot of his time and maybe if you are like Ben, with a big thing for learning but not for school, you should be left alone to do things your own way. That's what I thought lying there on Ben's floor after my alchemy lesson. I also didn't care about Soeur Rosa anymore and I probably wouldn't bother with her, I'd just keep this information for myself. This Grail business is a lot more interesting than I realized at first. A lot more.

It's getting dark outside and it's dark in Ben's room, a dark of another sort, and I can see it is starting to snow, and I have a good fierce feeling in my heart being right here in Ben's room and watching the snow come down outside in that featherweight way, like it's not sure whether to go right ahead and turn into a snowstorm or just flutter down for a little while in quiet flakes.

"Hey, Ben. I think Mum is Duplex. Get my 'rift?"

Ben says, "Got your 'rift." Ben has been telling me this sort of thing about Mum for years and I just want him to know I understand now.

"And you know what? I think Dad is a bit like King Arthur. All the knights sit around with him at the Round Table and people wander in, damsels and stags and other knights and so on and say, bring me the head of so and so, or, please rescue the damsel who is stuck in a castle with a lot of other damsels, or, come and cure the sick Fisher King—"

"Sick due to the opposites problem," Ben reminds me.

"Right! Got it. And anyway then King Arthur says, Okay, everyone off, go and heal the land or whatever, bring back the Grail, save the lady and so on and they all rise up at once and bash off on horseback, just like that. No one goes, well, I'm in the middle of something right now, King, do you think I could go in the morning? Or, I am a bit tired, can I have a snooze first? No. They just go. Arthur says, go forth, and all the knights jump to it. And Dad says, in the middle of a blizzard, go forth and bring me smoked-meat sandwiches and knishes from the deli, and off we go, remember that, Ben, when there wasn't a bloody car or a human being anywhere in sight and we fought our way to the deli, remember that? We could have died out there."

"Yup."

"And setting the table. This drives me crazy. Why does he need the table set two hours before dinner is even ready? It's like a state of emergency in the house and he goes stomping around, yelling, table-setters! Table-setters! Like he has this huge need to see the table set no matter what anyone is up to. It takes three and a half minutes to do and he is just standing around with Mum in the kitchen, why can't he reach in the drawer and haul out some knives and forks and napkins and glasses and just shuffle them out on the table? Why?"

"Maybe in his house they didn't have a proper dinnertime, I don't know," says Ben, "so now he wants it done right or something."

"Maybe they all ate standing up. Maybe they had no cutlery and just leaned up against each other eating bagels," I suggest.

"Stale ones," adds Ben. "With nothing in them."

Suddenly I hear the stomping tread of my dad. No one else walks like that and you can hear it several floors away and you just know he is coming for you, he wants one of his kids to do something for him. He is coming our way. I do a World War II commando roll and scoot under Ben's bed with seconds to spare. Dad pushes Ben's door open. He never knocks because it is his house and he does not have a big thing for knocking on doors.

"Ben! Have you seen Jem? I need a table-setter," my dad announces.

"She was here a moment ago. Don't know, Dad. Sorry."

"Okay. Well, tell her if you see her. And open a window in here. It smells of old socks."

"The archetype of the Old Socks!" I say from under the bed and I am getting a helpless giggly feeling now, due to not breathing for two minutes and foxing my dad.

"The archetype of the Slave Driver," says Ben.

"Ben. Dad is the Fourth man."

"Definitely," says Ben.

"Should we tell Mum?"

"She knows."

I roll out from under Ben's bed. "I better bloody set the bloody table, bloody. I hope I remember how to do it. It's so long since last night. Bloody. Hey, he didn't even think to ask you."

"I'm too important. I'm the eldest."

"Right. Well why can't Gus do it?"

"Too young. Too cute to do any work."

"Harriet then."

Ben says, "Too crazy. Cutlery all over the table in weird patterns."

"Jude could do it for once," I say.

"He's on drugs."

"He is?"

"He's smoking hash just about every afternoon. You haven't noticed at supper? His eyes are all red and he stares in the distance and eats and doesn't talk or answer anyone, you think that's normal?" asks Ben.

"Yeh, I do." I get up to leave Ben's room.

"I'll come with you," says Ben.

"You will? Like not even to help, just to be with me?"

"Yup."

"BROTHER-SISTER ARCHETYPE!" I hover at the door and Ben says,

"Archetype of the Doorknob."

I nod gravely and we travel on downstairs and I say, "Whoa! I smell lamb. Archetype of Lamb!"

"*Agnus Dei*," says Ben. "Paschal lamb. Lamb to the slaughter."

"Mary had a little lamb!" I say.

"Beh-eh-eh-eh," says Ben.

"Beh-eh-eh-eh. Time for Harriet to freak out. There is going to be some *obscurus* to behold, some bloody arcane substance in the final operations for sure," I say. "Archetype of Crazy Sister!"

"Archetype of Shut-up!" says Ben, and we burst into the kitchen, not surprising Mum at all.

When dinner is just about ready to happen and most of us are in the dining room, which is painted an exciting smudgy kind of blood-red, like when you look right down into the heart of a glass of red wine from above, something I love to do; when everyone has just about settled in and the last things are coming from the kitchen and even Jude has sat down, because he is always late now, I think about a chapter I finished reading in the Grail book Ben lent me. It has to do with the first time Perceval visits the Fisher King in the Grail Castle and this big procession happens right before Perceval's eyes and he is too stunned to ask any questions about it all, he is still too inexperienced and caught up with this idea of chivalry and he is not ready to ask the big question, he is not fully aware of things and this is his mistake, and why he has to bash off again and have a lot of perils before coming back to the Castle and healing the King and so on. This time, before the great dinner produced by the power of the Grail and featuring hind with pepper sauce and a lot of fine wine and anything anyone desires, he watches the procession of objects: a precious sword, a bleeding lance which sheds a drop of blood, and then the Grail itself, which is brought in by a beautiful damsel, and the Grail is so bright it obscures the candlelight in the room. Then a table comes in and a carving platter and two knives and all these things have big meanings, but Perceval has to have the experience before he can figure everything out and I don't blame him for that, although others did. That was unfair, I think. When you are on a big quest, the biggest of all, you should be allowed to mess up a little.

I look over at Jude who has slipped into his seat and I realize that only Jude and I take up the same places all the time, not that it's a rule or anything, it just happens that way. Mum and Dad sit at either end and for some reason my dad's place is called the head of the table but Mum's place is the end. I sit at one corner to Mum's left and Jude sits diagonally opposite at Dad's left. He always does. Once in a while Gus will climb onto that seat, out of dreaminess, but as soon as he sees Jude coming along, he remembers and slides right off and onto the next chair and no words are exchanged at all. Harriet, if she is being bloody, might perch in mine and she will be there, upright like a ballet dancer, and look everywhere but at me, her ponytail flipping around, just daring me to make a move on her. It's extremely annoying and it takes me quite a while to settle down in a different seat. But it's okay in the end, and Harriet does not do this very often.

Everyone drinks wine now except Gus who is still too young and Harriet who gets drunk just being close to a glass of wine, and on this night I sip the wine and I look all around at us in the blood-red room, I look at all the faces in my family and the procession of things and I think maybe Perceval felt like this on his first visit to the Castle, kind of thrilled and confused all at once, with an urge to ask some big question but holding back, with an urge to perform some act but not knowing what, and so maybe getting a little drunk instead, to fill that space he felt inside him, where electrical charges were going off, even though he did not know what electricity was, drinking from his golden goblet to feed that space where all the clamor was, everything shifting in alarm like before a storm.

．　　　．　　　．

Cup, chalice, goblet, glass, flûte, vessel, grave, Grail, uterus, soul, stone. I own beautiful glasses for drinking wine from. Blood, poison, balm, *obscurus.* They are dead simple but finely designed by some possessed Austrian who believes different wines should flow into and over different parts of you because they thrill in different ways. Okay. Cool with me. But like all things to do with the spirit, it is a private game, to be played in secret, like making a wish on your birthday cake with an upside-down knife. Two silver knives, broken sword, bleeding lance, Mover of Blood, Dolorous Stroke. Stop it.

When Perceval sees the Grail it releases a wonderful melody and a heavenly perfume. What is a heavenly perfume? The best thing you can wish to smell, I guess. Burgundy, peony, extramature cheddar on toast, autumn, loved one, loved ones.

Goddamn fucking-bloody bottle of Bowmore, right at the back of the cupboard now, each month pushed a bit farther out of sight, like Jem in dark times, your not-daughter, any place she lives too far for you to ride. Fatherless. So what. Here is an element of the hero myth. Perceval is fatherless. Of course he had a dad, maybe his dad loved him like crazy, yet Perceval grew up without him, fatherless, and so he has to compensate and develop a big thing for heroism, he has to be a hero for two and when you try to be a hero for two, you are liable to mess up. And another thing. Perceval comes from a line of kings; you have to be that way when you are the Grail hero even if you don't know it, that you have this royal blood in you. Maybe it is better if you don't know. It's not so cool to be royal, it doesn't do all that much for you. Look at the Fisher King, wounded in both thighs, not fit for anything but fishing in brooks, in the middle of a Wasteland, waiting for Perceval, who took one entire summer to find the Castle for the second time and then only stumbling into it by accident. Messing up again.

A person can get sick of a heavenly perfume. I don't know. You just stagger around, half-drunk on it like a kid learning to walk, when each step has one aim only, which is to stop him from falling over, and this is true of all locomotion, I guess, at any age, walking, running, dancing, wanderlust. Don't fall down. Keep moving.

Before the end of that summer, the summer when Jude read with his eyes closed and Ben drank out in the middle of the lake and Gus fished and fished like a demon and battled with asthma, I had my drink with Jude, in the city.

I am going back to school in eight days, everyone is, and so we have moved out of the cottage which we will now only see at weekends and we have bustled into town to shop for books we'll need and pens and pencils, just the right kind, not any old kind, each one of us having predilections when it comes to stationery, and we have to update our uniforms, checking out that everything matches, that no one is missing socks and there are enough perky-looking white shirts without ink stains or fraying cuffs for Weiss 3, 4 and 5. Weiss 1 is Ben and he is going to college and is no longer in a uniform situation. Jude is at a school now where you can wear anything you like just about.

I walk along with Weiss 2, that is Jude, and we are on our way to the café where he is going to buy me a drink. He walks on the outside of the pavement like Mum taught all the boys although Ben forgets and when he is out walking with you, he crosses all over in front and behind you, from one side to the other in a crazy fashion because he is usually pretty excited and talking about some wild topic and simply cannot organize himself to be a medieval gentleman and walk on the edge of the pavement to protect you from splashes and so on. Also, his legs are so long it is hard for him to stay with you, so he has to change his pace all the time. Things are complicated for Ben.

Jude, though, always walks slowly, even when he is in a hurry, and actually I think it is an accident that today he walks between the cars and me, out there on the edge. I think his memory of what Mum taught him is haphazard, like a lot of things with Jude. Gus is the one who always remembers and he is too young, but I can see how good he is going to be at all this, how easily it will come to him, how he will perform all these little tasks of opening doors and pulling out chairs and unfurling umbrellas without making a girl feel he is making a point of it and the girl will feel happy about this, she really will.

Wearing leather shoes and having combed hair and a tucked-in top feels peculiar after the wild freedom of summer, bare feet and hanging-out clothes and tangly locks and sunburn, and suddenly I tug at Jude's sleeve as we saunter along because I catch a scent of something in the air that is no longer summer but not yet autumn, something else, maybe just change, maybe that is all it is. It's exciting and scary at the same time and I have nothing to say but I do pull at Jude who knows what I mean by it and he nods and says, mmmn, quite slowly, in that way he has.

I have always wanted to come here, to this café-bar with tables outside and an inner courtyard with a glass roof and cool music and so on. This is the place I hear Ben and Jude mention on the phone to friends. I'll be at the Annexe, they say. I'll see you at the Annexe. Now I'm at the Annexe. I am here with Jude and he orders for us both, a specific type of beer, a glass for me, no glass for him. It's quite early but I look all around and the place is lively with voices and laughs and where there are just guys together there is backslapping and friendly cuffs on the shoulder, like a special language they have. It gives me a good feeling.

Jude pours for me, he doesn't let the bar guy do it, he pours for me carefully, tilting the glass so I get some foam but not too much. "Joe's coming later," he says.

"Now? When?" Not yet, Joe. Not yet.

"Later. You like Joe."

"Yeh," I say, meaning it. I don't want to disappoint Jude, but this is my drink with Jude and I want it to be just us, for a minute.

"Jem. I'm going away for a while," Jude announces, staring right at me so I feel a rush of prickles in my chest.

"What do you mean away, when, you can't, you have to go to school," I tell him.

"No, Jem. I'm taking a year off."

"Where are you going?"

"Shanghai, Kuala Lumpur, Goa, Delhi, Tehran, I don't know, Jerusalem for sure, Cairo first then Istanbul, maybe Athens and I'll end up at home, well, our old home, and I'll fly back here from there probably, I'll see, I'm not sure yet. I'll take pictures of the house for you, I could sneak over the fence into the garden, okay?"

I don't want pictures of our old house. What would I do with them. I do a frantic search in my mind for Shanghai and Goa and Tehran and I can't place them on a map. They are on no map I can imagine. Don't go.

"What about Christmas?" I ask, real pathetic now.

"I don't know, Jem. I probably won't make it, you know."

"How will I write to you? Are you going by yourself?"

"I'll write in advance with Poste Restante addresses. Hey, there's Joe." Jude waves him over. "Joe's flying to San Francisco with me, then we'll separate. Hey, Joe."

Joe is very nice always, he pays me a lot of attention but he speaks to me in a formal way like I am Audrey Hepburn and sometimes I wish he'd just cuff me on the shoulder like he does with Jude, although not so rough. He asks me if I would like another beer even though he can plainly see I have only had four sips and I say no thank you like I am Audrey Hepburn in a bad mood and I wonder what language we are speaking, why none of the words any one of us is saying matches the feelings or even the thoughts we are having. I want to leave the Annexe, I want to run right out of here, but instead I ask Jude, "What is Poste Restante, what is that?"

Jude explains and as soon as it does not seem too weird, I tell the guys I have to go, I promised Mum I'd help her with dinner and stuff, I've got to run and when I am out of sight, even though they are probably not even looking in my direction at all but talking about strange places in hot countries, I do run, I run the length of three whole bus stops, I run until my eyes have cleared and until my feet hurt too much due to my hard autumn shoes which are cutting up my wild summer feet, and now I have had my drink with Jude who is only 478 days older than I am but already so far away.

. . .

It's late and I am thinking about sleep. I mean I am thinking about the issue of sleep. I am not sleepy. Never mind. I am full of beta waves which are the waking waves. I remember this thing about sleep, that different animals have different sleep-type requirements, that predators get the most winks and prey get the fewest winks, practically no winks at all due to the need for perpetual alertness and the desire to stay alive and kicking, and not scarfed down in just a few ugly chomps by some dozy predator. It seems especially gruesome to have to live this way when your enemy is getting so much sleep but these are the facts. He can sneak up on you any old time and you have to be ready to run. I am not in any one of the sleep stages. Stages 1 and 2 are the least vital for the human brain. Little alpha waves come at this time, inducing drowsiness. Then comes Stage 3 and the beginning of delta waves when things start to dip, heart rate, blood pressure, arousal. Nearly there. In Stage 4 dreaming begins and you are all out dreaming in Stage 5, REM time, and your body is just about paralyzed and you can go through all these stages again and again in a night, although REM gets longer and longer, making me think that sleep is a daily quest, a journey as startling as the one I have now made across the Atlantic, brought here for a summer holiday twenty years after my first drink with Jude, transported by the power of my dad who is Rex, a ruler, and Mum who is Duplex, a magician.

Downstairs, Mum may be sleeping but I do not think so. She is worried about me and does not go in for sleep much. My dad sleeps. I know this because I can hear him, his subterranean snores like some terrible warning to the world, a message I dare not decipher.

Even in his realm of sleep, my dad is King. Do not wake him. Step lightly. My heart flutters at the crest of each snore as I sit cross-legged on my childhood summer bed, in the largest bedroom in our cottage, the room that was Ben's and in time became mine and then a guest room. I laugh softly. I am a guest in my old room. The carpet is creamy-white and it glows a little in the dark and there are sheets of Swiss lace at the balcony window which flow toward me now and again in the slight breeze, like a shy person trying to make an entrance. Come on in, goddamnit. Be my guest. Be a guest with me. Have a glass of wine. Cup, chalice, Grail.

Sleep. Gawain had a sleep disorder, I am pretty sure about it. He came so close to the Grail, even remembering to ask the big question, something Perceval forgot to do that first time. Gawain falls asleep when the Fisher King begins to explain the Grail mystery. Narcolepsy. Gawain nods off in the big moments and so he is doomed to a life of restlessness and knight-type adventures and not to sit in the *siège périlleux*. Maybe this was his choice. I think so. He had a way with chivalry, and although he tried real hard to reach the spiritual place for Arthur and the Round Table, it was not his big thing in the end. It was Perceval's big thing. Sleep. Merlin appears to Perceval and reminds him of a promise he made not ever to sleep twice in the same place until he finds the Grail. Keep moving, Perceval. Don't fall down.

Blood. In Malory's version, Perceval's sister is a big cheese and she is the one who points her brother toward the Grail, she is the unfurler of maps, the one with all the instructions, the right-hand man, it is not Merlin at all, but the thing is, she has to die for Perceval so he can get there, she has to satisfy some spooky custom at a castle on the way, involving a dish full of blood and it has to be hers because she is a maid and a king's daughter and so on. It just has to be hers and she faces the facts. "Who shall let me blood?" she asks, real cool, while all the guys are fighting it out, trying to sidestep the custom and save her. She dies in Perceval's arms and asks to be buried in the City of Sarras, that is Jerusalem, the *spiritual place* where she sends Perceval for the Grail. Before her lights go out she tells her brother he will also be buried there, and she is right about that. Sir Bors buries Perceval right alongside her and not long after he has achieved the Grail and dropped out of the world, opting for higher things and letting everyone down back home at the Round Table where the perilous seat stayed empty, the one only he should be warming up with the heat of all his virtue and knowledge and big-time grasp of spiritualities. Perceval, perilous boy, fatherless, royal, piercer of valleys, man without maps, what happened out there?

Blood. There is a big knife right here on the bed with me and it looks gruesome and silly at the same time, a B-movie item, oh yes, and I laugh again. It's a night full of laughs. No blood, Jem. Not in your father's house, not in this royal place. I wish Ben were here, my restless knight, adventure-seeker, uneasy man, I wish he were here to talk alchemy to me and lighten things up with science, all the mysteries that bring a person down, and he'd remind me that drops of blood, *obscurus*, will fall not in threes as uptight Christians will have you believe, but in fours because you cannot leave the devil out. Quaternity. I like this word.

Creamy carpet. Red and white, Ben told me once, are classical alchemical colors. I remember this, and they represent the masculine and feminine, and need to go together. Blood on snow. When Perceval leaves the Grail Castle that first time without having asked the big question, due to extreme youth and inexperience, he runs into a cousin of his and she is really mean to him. "You didn't ask the question? What an idiot! And guess what?" she adds, "your mother is dead and you killed her. You thought she was just fainting from grief or something when you rode away? Nope. Curtains. You killed her. Well done."

No one needs a cousin like this.

Perceval staggers off into the forest real depressed now and has a rotten night and in the morning he sees a falcon attacking some little birds and blood falls on the new snow and this vision sends him into an actual frozen state and he just sits on his horse dreaming, and this makes me think of Jude and how he could read with his eyes closed. Pretty soon Gawain comes along to see what's up and Perceval wakes all enlightened, the blood on the snow being a big sign for him, something to do with suffering and soul-type problems, feminine things he had lost touch with. It's complicated for Perceval. Questing is a hard job, it really is.

I have an urge to go outside and I slip my feet into black plimsolls and haul on an old sweatshirt of Jude's I found in the cupboard. I pour more wine and lay a Kleenex over the glass so nightflies don't go for a swim in it, then I snigger, finding some more mirthful things in this hilarious night. In the most reckless times, you can be so fastidious. Don't drip on the white carpet. Keep warm. Don't swallow any bugs. Walk softly.

I don't clamber over the roof or anything, I take Jude's old advice regarding late-night exits and go right out the front door onto the terrace and I sit on the wrought-iron chair and settle my wine next to the bust of a young man's head that Mum placed on the stone wall at the edge of the terrace, on top of this hill that rises above the lake. All her little monuments and statues are judiciously placed and sometimes you run slap into them when you don't expect it. There are sexpot cherubs all over the joint, poking out of the bushes, lolling in flower beds, but this guy is a prize. He is kind of mournful but determined and has real delicate features and, goddamnit, he looks like Jude and he is facing out, his thoughts are seabound. The spirit in the stone. Perilous boy.

I reach forward and pat him on the head and I rest my feet up on the wall and look at the water which is shimmering now in the starlight. It's pretty cool. When you are a little kid and you want to scare yourself with big ideas, open-mouth-screaming type horrors, this is what you rustle up. Death; yours, Mum's. Pollution, nuclear war. When you are a bit older, not much, you picture gruesome accidents such as walking right into the jaws of a boa; helping your Mum in the kitchen and losing all your fingers in a whirl of food-processor blades; landing in a fox trap and having your foot lopped off; blithely stepping into a lift on the eighteenth floor, a lift which is not there. Yikes. But here is what you do not imagine, you do not imagine standing in the middle of Ben's old room late at night when you are a grown-up and being so aware of his absence it is like being winded. You do not foresee lying on the dock in the hot afternoon, when you know you are the only Weiss visiting home on this day, and you jerk around suddenly expecting Jude, or Gus the Fisher King, just because the dock lurches in its moorings and the chains rattle, but it is only a passing wave, the wake of a speedboat, that is all. You do not expect to pick some old book off the childhood shelf, some old book about King Arthur, and see your own name in the flyleaf, in handwriting you accept as yours but that you no longer recognize and could not reproduce and the gulf between you and you is something terrible, like a sea of dragons. So these are a few open-mouth-screaming type horrors you do not imagine when you are a little kid.

I slink down into the chair, raising my knees, and I tilt my head back and stare up at stars. Harriet says, the harder you stare at the night sky, the more the stars will come out for you and she is right of course, she knows about this sort of thing.

"Harriet," I say. "Ben, Jude, Gus." Everything is so funny tonight.

You never did make it home that Christmas, Jude, which is more or less what you said when you took me for my drink, it's what you said but I kept thinking you might appear and I actually cupped my eyes with my hands against windows to see out into the night, in case maybe at that moment you would be trudging up the snowy driveway with your heavy hockey bag full of dusty clothes and exotic things from hot places, ready to dump it at our feet indoors, in that triumphant coming-home type way. Thud goes the bag. Here I am. I expected you until way past the last minute and I jumped at telephone rings and slamming doors and I decided that everyone but me knew you were coming and that it was a surprise, a conspiracy, and I was proud of this fine acting job everyone in the Weiss family was doing.

Gus sorted out the Christmas lights due to his expertise with all things electrical and his breath went in and out like a sharp wind whistling against buildings and trees and his chest crackled like a dying fire, but he never said a word about it and you had to respect that. It was the worst year for him though, and at times he scared us, he really did.

It was pretty late on Christmas Eve and Ben and I had the table to do. Harriet might have helped but after spending about eight hours wrapping one single present out of the thirteen she was supposed to wrap, covering it with tiny cut-out animals she had drawn and attaching a lot of bows and stars and stuff to it, she was knocked out. She had one half-sip of champagne and announced she was drunk.

"I am definitely drunk. Mummy, I'm drunk," Harriet said in that special shocked voice of hers, like she had just seen the worst thing of all, a dead deer on the road or something.

"Why don't you go for a little walk in the snow and take some DEEP BREATHS!" says Mum, not all that worried and very busy with stuffing and stock and turkey and so on. Mum is really into deep breaths but Harriet says maybe she should just go to bed which is what she does, but not before Ben and I give her long suspicious stares with half-lowered eyelids, meaning, Harriet walks off the job again. There she goes. Never mind.

Ben and I are deep into the champagne. It's a good feeling. Ben is busy carving skinny tapers to fit the black iron candle holders Mum found in some Scandinavian place and for which no candles in the Western world are made to fit, so every year someone has this job of carving tapers. Mum has a habit of buying unusual, elegant objects that do not belong in the regular world, such as hand-painted Italian writing-pad holders for which no replacement pads are made anywhere and each Weiss kid gets the shopping job of looking for a replacement pad for about as long as he lives because no such thing exists. It's weird, but we all keep looking for her. It's hard to say no, you don't want to let her down.

Another laugh, Jem. On this single night, on Christmas Eve, Jem is the one with the mania for table-setting, I am the one insisting on having this table set some eighteen hours before Christmas dinner is ready and my dad comes into the dining room and asks why don't I leave it until tomorrow, go to bed? This is funny and I think about my dad that Christmas Eve and how he sauntered into rooms, filling up Mum's glass of champagne and maybe Ben's and mine too, although not without a dark look, wary of drunken youths, something he has no idea how to handle. And there he is, a bit bleary-eyed himself, sipping single malt and glancing around at us, maybe wondering what all the fuss is about and who are these people getting so busy and high, who are these big kids in his house, growing too big for a cowboy to corral, who are these bagel-eating carol-singing kids, a clash of knights keeping him up way past his bedtime?

Then my dad does this thing. I am polishing knives and glasses, smoothing white tablecloth, dancing around the table, messing with Ben still busy with candles, and Dad comes right up and pulls out the chair at the corner of the table, the one on the left of his place, Jude's seat.

"This will make more room," he says. "Ben can spread out a bit tomorrow."

My dad pulls the seat all the way out and places it against the wall and I am staring at him, I am split like a stone.

"Leave it! Don't do that! Put it back!" I scream, and I am so shocked by my own hysteria that I run out of the dining room and upstairs, vaguely aware of bewildered voices in my wake, and I lock myself in the bathroom and cry big old tears, hot and stingy with champagne and a lot of stuff I don't understand, and I do this until Mum comes for me and lures me back into the world with a gentle voice that somehow seeps into the chaos and melts it a little, like maybe warm blood on fresh snow.

. . .

A maid and a king's daughter, that's how it goes, but on this night full of jokes, there is no dish full of blood, how about that, and still I'm facing out with you and I try to see for you, I try to do this thing, this unfurling of maps. This is where we are. We are here.

When King Arthur and his knights learn that Perceval has won the Grail but will not be coming home, he will not be coming back to the Round Table to sit in the *siège périlleux*, the perilous seat that is now his own, that no one else can occupy, it is very big news and a calamitous moment because the knights know they have seen the last of Perceval and there is a gap in the circle and they will never be whole again. They have to break up and bash off on their own and try to be whole in their separate ways and they are not sure how to do this. Maybe they had seen it coming, I don't know, but when Perceval does not return, they grasp it for sure, this end of things, this start of something else, something they cannot picture. And this is what I read, that when the King and his knights heard the big news, these guys who jump up and embark on perils and adventures, no questions asked, going all out for chivalry, and dicing with death with the same lack of hesitation a person feels flicking on a light in a darkened room, when the King and his knights heard this, I read, "they began to weep with one voice."

NO TIME

There are no ghosts. That is the first thing you must remember. There are no ghosts, only physics and laws of chemistry and neurobiology and so on, that is all. But there is something in my room right now and I can't figure out what, although I am working on it and suddenly I wish I were a kid again in a time when you are supposed to be afraid of ghosts but are not in the least afraid of ghosts. I wish I were a kid again because I finally know exactly who I want to dress up as on Halloween, and that is Marley's Ghost, the anxious spirit of Jacob Marley, maybe the finest ghost of all, a big cheese ghost and a favorite character of mine in books. And Marley's Ghost is all science.

There is a basic law of physics I can recall, and my grasp of things scientific has always been faulty; the moment I have seized upon the bare physical reality of a science problem, I am a giddy kid on that first bike glide without training wheels and when I try to see just a little bit beyond this basic thing, this simple action and reaction, all I can conceive of is chaos and combustion, and that is like flying over the handlebars, a gruesome tangle of limbs, your body a pathetic wreck of bloody knees and elbows and a forlorn expression. You are supposed to keep trying. Why?

You are supposed to be learning about balance, I guess, and locomotion, but I never once saw Mum on a bicycle and I don't think she ever owned one, even as a little kid, and she has just about the most prizewinning balance and locomotive ability I have observed in a human. My dad is a bit tippy. He is not a bicycle rider, but I think it is just a thing with him. I would never ask him to pass me a glass of wine, for instance, even if he only has a straight path to walk toward me with no foxy objects underfoot or people in the way. He will get to me but there will be some wine strewn around between us and not a lot left in the glass. Never mind. It is a balance problem but I do not believe bike-riding would have helped him much. It is all science, though, everything. The cochlea is part of the inner ear and it is the organ of balance, and when the head moves, canals filled with fluid send impulses right on over to the brain which works hard to match these up with what the eyes are seeing and the legs and arms are feeling. It's a tough business and no amount of bike-riding will help you out if these parts of you are not up to the job. That's how it is.

So here is that basic law of physics, as far as I understand it anyway, this law of displacement, everything taking up some space that another thing once occupied. There is no emptiness. Something like that. I pour wine into my glass and the wine displaces the air that was sitting in there before and some of it now rushes up toward my face, mixing up with the volatile elements of the wine which is vapor now, rising through my nose to my olfactory bulb, nestled right in front of my temporal lobe where my memories are, and it shuffles them around maybe, starting something up, everything shifting, changing places. Everything gets pushed around, so let's say I rise right up from a prone position in bed because I think I have an uninvited guest in my room at four in the morning. What I am doing is pushing the air around and it has to shift elsewhere. Okay. And here is how it applies to so-called ghosts, for instance that remorseful spirit of Jacob Marley in *A Christmas Carol—A Ghost Story of Christmas*, written in 1843 by Charles Dickens and illustrated by John Leech in four etchings and four woodcuts.

When Ebenezer Scrooge gets home from his accounting firm, which still has his dead partner's name over the door along with his own, reading SCROOGE & MARLEY, he is in a pretty bad mood as usual, especially bad in fact, due to its being Christmas Eve, a time that can put a lot of people in a bad mood, even cheery types who are holding out for really good things to happen in their lives. It's that kind of time and it is hard to handle. Scrooge's first spooky moment comes when his door knocker turns into Jacob Marley's face. Yikes. It's possible Scrooge is merely hungry and hallucinating, I don't know. He is a miser and does not go in for the comfort of comestibles but once he settles in upstairs after another hallucination featuring a horse-drawn coach riding right up his staircase, he crouches next to a mean little fire in his cavernous grate, in an uncomfortable chair, and he gets ready to eat up some gruel. Lo! Here comes his ex-partner, who died seven Christmases ago.

Marley's Ghost walks right up to Ebenezer in a ramrod fashion and he is transparent, and that spooks Scrooge very badly. Also, he has stary eyes and a bandage wrapped around his head and tied in a neat bow under his chin, like it is holding his jaw in place or like he has an eternal toothache or something, and when he gets really mad at Ebenezer, he undoes it and his lower mandible clatters right down onto his chest. This would be a topmost important item in the Halloween costume I never wore; it has a lot of spook-power, this bandage.

The main costume feature however would be the chain Marley has draped around his waist, the one dragging on behind him with a lot of heavy metal bound to it, keys and locks and steel purses and so on, like a really bad news no-charm bracelet. Another habit Marley's Ghost has is to rattle this chain when he is very cross. Ebenezer makes him very cross. Here is why, and it is also the science part. "I wear the chain I forged in life," is what Jacob says, and it is a key piece of information, a warning to Ebenezer who has become a foul man, a man with a mangy little heart and no time for anyone and not one single fine thing to say at any moment. Ebenezer has a spirit problem and it is nearly too late for him. Jacob was the same way in life and now he is going to save Scrooge because that is his job. Because Jacob's spirit did not go forth in life, because it did not roam around in a warm-hearted way, because it withered and got trapped, now he is doomed to go walkabout for eternity with a lot of other lamenting ghosts, wailing and moaning and having a really bad time, flying through the cold night air, in a night without end, all due to having had mean and captive spirits in their lifetimes, ones that did not go into happy circulation amongst their fellow men, etc. It's a displacement thing and it's a chain reaction. Jacob left no good feelings behind, no one wanted a part of him in their memories, so he has to take up space in the afterlife, in the depressive dead department, and occasionally he gets to appear to a living person, particularly one hurtling toward a sorry end, and he moves into that person who then has to eject a lot of crabby feelings to make room within. Sometimes it works and sometimes not and Scrooge, for instance, is okay in the end. His spirit goes forth and so on. That's how I see it at four A.M.

So who is that in my room? A chain-rattler? Do I know you?

I have a big feeling for science right now in the middle of the night, at this time when the dead return, and I am kind of relieved because if you have a big feeling for science at four in the morning, you have a sort of hands on hips reaction to whatever it is that is lurking in your room. I think about the mechanics of fear. I remember a German film I once saw and the best thing was the title and the title was *Fear Eats the Soul*. Okay. I think it is true that fear is corrosive, but it is also galvanizing, it is a powerful tool, and has this kind of effect on a person in a danger situation, that you can be like some flopsy old puppet in bed and suddenly it is like your strings are yanked tight and you are charged up with electricity and you can do a lot of damage to the enemy, no matter what his size. Fear wakes the soul.

At my first convent when I was a little kid, Lord Nelson was held up as a big hero in history and they taught how Lord Horatio grew up not knowing the meaning of fear, like this was some fine thing and maybe there were no dictionaries in his house and he was too proud and bloody to go and ask his parents Mr. and Mrs. Nelson. But they got it wrong at my convent; of course he knew the meaning of fear, Nelson was a big hero because he knew how to let fear work for him, charging him up with electricity and the ability to perform heroics, and anyone who decided to sail through the waters he protected, anyone who bobbed on the oceans, guns poised and with bad intentions, even one-eyed and one-armed, Horatio could make them look silly. That's how it was.

The nervous system has its own engine which doesn't really depend on you to be all ready to use it, so in a way it is smarter than you and it has a mind of its own and that is why it is called autonomic, the autonomic nervous system, and it is divided into two parts, the sympathetic and the parasympathetic. I like this a lot, these are good words, and show just how your body can work for you if you understand it and are willing to hand over the reins now and again, like at four in the morning when you perceive some kind of danger and your mind wants to sleep through it. In a danger situation, the sympathetic part wakes you up, due to the fear in your sleepy head, it rouses you in all kinds of ways, raising the rate and strength of your heartbeat, dilating your pupils, widening the airways in your lungs, decreasing your digestive activities so more energy is freed up for whatever tussle you may have on your hands. It's a cool system but you have to get it right or you might let yourself get charged up all the time, like just because a little breeze plays over your face or the wooden frame of the big mirror in your bedroom contracts in the cold night, and then you are bound to be a sad mess of brain and neurological activity and you could fall apart and this brings me to that other basic law of physics that I remember from school. This law is called *la loi de Newton* and has to do with momentum and it is pretty useful in ways I never realized before. *La loi de Newton* is named after Sir Isaac Newton who was a Fellow of the Royal Society in the seventeenth century, a Christian society and a big-cheese center of scientific thought which had to conclude that the politics of Christianity simply got in the way of science and you just had to keep them apart. Not for

Isaac, though, who saw science everywhere, even in myth and faith and revelation, and he must have had a really big heart and champion type brain to see reason in things beyond understanding, and feel awe and magic in things he could take apart and put back together with logic and long, sensitive fingers.

Mme Beckers was the physics teacher at my French convent and we all liked her very much, all the girls did, and we would shuffle around in happy readiness when she came into the classroom, usually dropping a book or her handbag and maybe even tripping on something not there on her way to the desk, and no matter what the mishap, she'd be smiling, we'd all see this dozy smile of hers through the locks of very blond hair tumbling over her eyes. Mme Beckers is married to a Belgian. She often wears black bras under pink or white tops and you know this is because her home is a merry mess and she cannot find her light-colored bras, her house is in big-hearted disarray because Mme Beckers spends her time correcting physics homework and thinking about physics and cooking for M. Beckers and throwing her arms around people near to her and getting pregnant, as she was in my one and only year of physics. I liked Mme Beckers and due to my good feeling for her, I can recall some basic laws of physics that are helping me out in dark times.

Here is the example Mme Beckers gave us to illustrate *la loi de Newton*. You are riding on a bus and you are standing up, hopefully holding on to a bar, you are standing up because there are no seats left, or you have given up your seat in a fine Christian manner to: a cotton top, or/person with big-time shopping/person with small child/person with walking stick/person who is not yet a cotton top but is a lot older than you and is in a very sad mood. Or maybe you just feel like standing up. Okay. The bus is getting close to stopping at a bus stop or red traffic light. It stops. You keep moving. Your body is still on its way in the bus direction but your guts have stayed behind. That is all due to Newton's law, the one to do with momentum, and if you are on a bus with a bus conductor, you will find some of them know this law well, having seen a lot of passengers careen toward the front of the bus, limbs akimbo, tipping forward like soldiers climbing out of trenches into gunfire and falling right over in a terrible heap. That is why a nice bus conductor will say hold tight before the bus moves and before it aims to stop. A not nice conductor, one with a tired old stringy heart and bleak feelings, will say nothing at all and just gaze out of the window, and he is usually a change-rattler too. He has one hand filching around in the weight of change in his pocket and he rattles the coins without mercy. He will also find the one passenger who hates this sound a lot, a person for whom the sound is blood-curdling as a war cry, and he will step right up to that person and do a lot of heavy change-rattling while gazing out of the window. He picks me. This is the chain I forged in life. Clang, clang, rattle.

Hold on tight. When you are in a state of anxiety, next stop fear, last stop terror, all change, please, then I think the mind goes on this journey, hurtling forward with a desire to stop but nothing to grab on to. Adrenaline is rushing through your body, putting you in this state of alarm and readiness, something they call the fight-flight response. It is a response we share with wild animals and it is very useful but can take you too far, propelling you into a place you cannot picture and may not survive, so this is when I find it useful to remember Mme Beckers and *la loi de Newton*. A formula went with it but I cannot summon that up, that is an over the handlebars moment, one struggle too many. I do recall the basic physical action and reaction, though, and I say to myself, Hold tight. Find something to kill the speed. A good joke, a bit of science, something, because where you are heading, if you do not kill the speed, is a place worse than right here with a shape in your room shaking a long and heavy coil, raising an almighty cry, this soul in exile, displaced spirit, someone you might just reason with, taking another fine tip from Sir Isaac who could wring a formula right out of a revelation, who could map the divine.

Giving up the ghost. Give up, ghost! Who are you? Can you— can you sit down? Grave, gravitas, gravity, Newton, hold tight, step on the brakes. Halloween, a night I never knew what to wear. Jacob Marley. Slowing down now. Parasympathetic nervous system in gear. Heart slowing. The heart is a pump with four chambers. There are no ghosts, I don't think so. In my mind's eye. The pupil is an opening in the center of the iris. Light enters it. In darkness, the pupil dilates. Did you say something? My inner ear contains two organs. The cochlea is my organ of balance, my organ of hearing is a labyrinth.

Whoa. Ben is really mad at me.

Here is what Ben shouts at me. "YOU ARE STUCK IN THE PAST! YOU KNOW NOTHING ABOUT LIFE! YOU ARE WALKING ABOUT IN THE NINETEENTH CENTURY! LA-DE-DAH! YOU DON'T KNOW THE FIRST THING ABOUT SCIENCE! YOU DON'T EVEN TALK LIKE A MODERN PERSON! YOU READ AND READ AND YOU DON'T KNOW ANYTHING! YOU THINK THE SUN IS THE MOON AT NIGHT! WAKE UP!"

Bloody.

Actually I did think the Sun turned into the Moon at night until quite recently and I am fourteen now. Okay. At least I owned up, unlike some. Mum used to read this book to us when we were little kids and it was called *The Sun Our Nearest Star* and that did it, I got confused for life. What do you mean a star? Stars are little things. I don't know. Anyway, I think being accused of living in olden times is not fair coming from Ben, my brother with a big thing for candelabra and black capes with red lining and a fear of naked electricity shining out of bulbs, which is what most of us are used to by now. And all because I said this thing to Jude, who was lying on the floor with closed eyes, a book he is supposed to be reading for school open on his stomach. He rose up and stretched like a mountain lion and told me he was going to the kitchen for a snack. Jude needs snacks quite often to feed his brain which does a lot of thinking although this might not be your very first idea about him if you are a stranger and passing by, it might seem to you that he does a lot of sleeping but this would be the wrong idea to have. And this is what I said to Jude which made Ben scream at me about being stuck in the past.

I said, "I wish you Godspeed," which is a thing I say to Jude.

My dad also knows some expressions which are maybe not regular ones. For instance, if he claps eyes on you and you happen to be doing something idiotic, let's say, licking a knife because there is sauce or cheese on it that is too good to waste, he will shout at you, "Don't put a knife in your mouth, you knucklehead!" And then he might bash you on the skull with a rolled-up newspaper. What is a knucklehead? I don't know. It is some olden times word I have never heard a single other human being utter. Here is another thing he says quite a lot, like if he sees we are about to be late for school, or are dawdling around avoiding some job like raking leaves or homework, we are just loitering in the kitchen thinking about snacks or fingering books, etc., he will shove us in the shoulder area and say, pretty loud, "Come on! Move it! Make tracks!"

Make tracks must be an olden times expression from the days in my dad's country when there were Native Indians sniffing around in the snow, tracking white men and animals in no time at all due to special wisdom in a tracking situation. Usually my dad wants us out of the house so he can be alone with Mum, even just to watch her do stuff, anything, because she is his all-time favorite person and puts him in a pretty good mood. And sometimes he just clears us right out of the house and away from her, suddenly, like there is an air raid on or something.

My dad took Ben, Jude, Harriet and me to the cinema to get us out of Mum's way one Christmas. He shoved us in the shoulders and slammed caps on our heads and yelled, "Move it! Make tracks!" and soon we were all piling into our light-blue Renault. Mum needed time without us, she had to do a lot of cooking plus looking after Gus, who is no trouble at all and really smart and wise, I think, even then when he was barely in the world and still wobbly on his feet and speaking only two words, "Oh dear," which he says exactly the way Mum does, kind of soft and gentle even in the face of calamity such as broken things or spilled stuff or very loud noises. Gus repeats it after her, "Oh dear," and these are good words these first words of his, they can suit a lot of situations, and even pass as a greeting and that's what I mean when I say he is wise.

This film Dad took us to see was called *One Million Years B.C.* and there is a scene in it when all the cavemen and cavewomen are huddled around a huge fire and yelling and croaking at each other in prehistoric language and hauling great ugly bites off the biggest chicken legs you've ever seen, dribbling and choking, food bits flying out of their jaws, the cave types making a pretty bad mess of things. It was a really annoying film, the only kind my dad takes us to, and during this scene my dad starts laughing his big laugh and his shoulders are shaking and his hair is flopping around like he is on a bumper-car ride at a fun fair.

He says right out loud in the cinema, "It's just like our house at suppertime! Ha ha ha!" Then there were some grown-up laughs out there in the audience, like they were saying to my dad, yeh, we have that at home too, clumsy cavekids slinging food around, ha ha ha.

It was pretty embarrassing.

Ben says, "Jem, you need to know about science and you need to read some books set in now-time not just the way-off past, you have to. Okay?"

"Yeh," I say, in an okay I give up voice. "Why though?"

"You won't understand the world and you have to."

"Oh. But I can't do science, I can't do sums, you have to be good at sums, I hate that, it gives me a headache."

"I can't do sums but I know a thing or two about science. It's not good at school but I have books and Mum is really good at science stuff, she knows some really weird things," says Ben.

"Because Mum is weird in a nice way, right; she is descended from Druids, right? A white witch, right?"

"Right."

"And she is really good at everything," I add. "Except maybe sports. Hey, have you ever seen Mum kick a football, have you, Ben? What does it mean?"

"Her nice shoes?" suggests Ben. "No. She doesn't like to make sudden moves, that must be it."

I think about this and it is true, all Mum's movements are cool to watch like listening to classical piano music, not the noisy stuff but the sad spooky stuff that is beautiful I think, the way Mum is.

"Yeh," I say. "That must be it. Or else she is really good at football and doesn't want to make you feel bad about your own messy kicks of balls. I bet that's true too, what do you think, Ben?"

"Yeh, probably."

"So what am I supposed to read?" I ask. "To be in now-time."

"I'll find some stuff for you later. And why do you say that anyway, 'I wish you Godspeed,' what is that?"

"It's just a joke. It's a joke I do with Jude. You had to be there, I can't explain it. It's like us, we have jokes that Jude won't get."

The truth is I am pretty worried about olden times, I am mixed up about them, I don't know if things were better then or just different, and mostly I can't see how we grew out of them, I don't recognize anything much in cavemen or very old paintings, etc., and so I need to figure things out although there are whole parts of history, such as prehistory, I am not interested in at all except for this thing I learned about table manners and how in this, according to my dad, we are not so far apart from cave types. Maybe I am just looking too hard for a connection, maybe there is no chain at all between then and now and I should just get over it and relax in now-time, I don't know.

This is why I say I wish you Godspeed to Jude. I have this rule about words and it is the Three Times or More rule and it means if I see a word I don't know three times or more then I will have to go look it up or ask someone, usually Mum, Dad or Ben depending on how much I want to know and what kind of information I am after. And here is someone not to ask about a word unless it is a bit dodgy. Jude.

I am in a pretty lazy mood and Jude and I are lying around in the afternoon reading books. I have seen this expression I wish you Godspeed about eighteen times but I do not think it is a proper word at all, Godspeed, so my rule does not work, I don't use the rule and I ask Jude to explain it because I think this is some olden times word and he knows about olden times, we read the same books featuring medieval knights and World War I and World War II soldiers and these things involve a special language.

"Jude," I say. I don't make it a question or else he might take about three weeks to answer me so I say "Jude" in a warning way, like I am about to speak, please listen, etc. "Jude, what is Godspeed, what is that, 'I wish you Godspeed'?"

I keep coming across this not only in books with knights and soldiers but in television programs set in olden times. Usually the person saying it hugs the other one in a big man hug which men do all the time in the past, and the one saying it will slap the horse's flank if his friend is about to bash off on horseback, or it might be a motorcycle if it's World War I. Same words, I wish you Godspeed.

"Dunno," says Jude.

"Come on, you must know. Is it a special speed, Godspeed, you can go as fast as you like, no crashing, fast like wind or the speed of light or something, that's the fastest, right, the speed of light? I mean, it's an olden times version, this Godspeed, very very fast with no crashing due to God watching and looking out for you, is that it?"

"Yeh."

"You're just saying that, you're not even listening!"

"I am, I think you're right," says Jude, rolling over on his back and raising his book up in the air, like a sea lion at the zoo.

"Well, if that's it, you can't say it now, it's embarrassing, only for nuns and stuff. I bet my nuns believe in Godspeed, yeh. Bloody. Like Immaculate Conception, they believe that too. Face the facts, I want to tell them."

"Yeh," says Jude, like he is definitely not listening but the thing is, one day he'll repeat it all back to me, everything I said, like he hears but he puts all the words away later, like when he helps out with the shopping and then dumps the bags in the hall because he is tired and you have to leave it for him and not put it away, he has to do it but in his own time, Jude-time.

Here is one thing I know was worse in olden times and that is the birth situation. In fact I can't understand how there were any people at all seeing as every time there is a drama with costumes on TV, the mother is giving birth and there is a lot of torture-like screaming and about five or six people holding her in place, and if she isn't dead by the end of it, the little kid is, so where did all those people come from? I read about this childbirth situation and it makes me cross, all that pacing up and down and whisky-drinking the men do if they care about the woman at all, or else, if they are poor and not all that smart, they just compare it to cows and horses in a barn and leave it up to Nature and God and so on which is pretty annoying. It also seems a very painful thing to do and I wonder if I will go in for childbirth when the time comes for me.

"The immaculate bit means no sex, dummy," Jude says.

"No, no. It's no sex, I know that, God, I'm not an idiot but I think it's the whole thing, you know, the birth part too."

Because most women were just flopping around in a bloody

death heap in a birth situation, when Gabriel showed up for Mary, holding up two fingers to represent the dual nature of Christ, as in all my favorite Renaissance paintings, when he said, this is how it's going to be, everyone needed this to be a safe birth situation and this meant no sex to get things under way and maybe a pillow inside Mary's dress so it looked like a regular baby growing and then a little fake screaming from Mary and a magic baby, no mess, no casualties at all. I explain this to Jude.

"I'd like to see you tell the nuns that," says Jude in a sneery way.

"Maybe I will."

"Sure," says Jude, getting up and stretching and letting out a big howly sound making me think about childbirth again. "I need a snack."

"I wish you Godspeed," I say to Jude. He grips both sides of the doorway and leans back, catapulting himself right out of the room, and he runs for the kitchen, which is not all that far away, but it is fun seeing Jude move quickly, not something he does much at all, practically never, usually only for a joke. It's weird, Jude walks at thought-speed, like when you have a tough problem to think out and your head gets hot and your body moves as if it were under water. When I think about him, he is always still, that is how I picture him, there is no motion but he is always going places, always somewhere else, and this is a weird thought.

I aim to read the books Ben gives me, the science ones and also novels with fast cars and electricity and washing machines and no sudden death in childbirth, books set in now-time and spacetime, because if I look at things with science eyes maybe I will be less confused, maybe I will get out of the past where Ben says I am stuck.

I sit up straight in science classes because sitting up straight and paying attention are supposed to go together, although I have my doubts about this, I don't think they are connected at all. I sit up straight just like Harriet. She always sits this way, even at suppertime, and does not pay attention to a single thing that is going on right in front of her unless she wants to. Never mind.

I am not very good at science, I am losing heart about it, but I keep hearing Ben and I sit up straight because sometimes if you try to be good at a thing for someone else, someone you are crazy about, and not just for yourself, you can do a bit better at it. Sometimes, not always. Soon I am going to get even worse at science due to Mme Beckers and the baby within. That baby is ready to come out and be with M. et Mme Beckers and make some more mess in their happy messy house. Soeur Rosa comes in to announce our replacement and I have a sinking feeling, I know whoever it is will be no match for Mme Beckers.

"Girls," says Soeur Rosa who reminds me of Mussolini. "You have a new physics teacher. Until Mme Beckers is better."

Soeur Rosa takes a little stroll in front of the classroom, arms folded and with a little Italian half-smile starting up on her face like an omen. I want to tell her Mme Beckers is not sick, she is having a baby and it was a regular-type conception with sex and everything.

"M. Kassovitz is a Jew," she says. I knew something was up. Another Jesus-killer, apart from me that is, and I am only half-Jewish. "Do not ask him any questions about religion, do you understand? Do not mention Jesus."

Bloody. What is wrong with this nun? First of all, what makes her think we are a gaggle of girls just itching to ask everyone questions about religion, maybe stopping passersby even, and asking them for the lowdown on the Trinity or transubstantiation instead of what we do ask, such as, do you have any matches? So we can light Gitanes, etc. Why would we ask him about religion in a physics class anyway? All she is doing is having another Jewish moment, letting us know M. Kassovitz is some kind of invalid and we all have to be very delicate and polite around him due to the Jewish situation wherein he is trapped, a situation of no salvation unlike where all the nuns and the rest of the girls are, a place of all-out salvation. Fucking-bloody, as Harriet would say.

One thing I have noticed is that unlike nuns, Jewish types do not have a big thing for talking about religion, and that is okay with me, except for some times when they just leave you in the dark, times when you do have questions and they walk out on you, types such as my dad, who is both halves Jewish, no messing around. One Passover night for instance, I am in the kitchen having a snack before dinner, chewing on a binocular roll, and he grabs it right out of my hand.

"Hey, Dad," I say, a bit startled. "Is this a game?"

"You can't have that tonight!" he says all flustered and cross, his hair flopping around.

"I'm hungry, Dad."

"It's leavened bread! You can't have it tonight! No! I mean it, Jem!"

"Why?" Cool your jets, Dad.

"When the Jews were in flight, they could only make unleavened bread. You can have matzoh!"

Okay. I am not that hungry. Matzoh is like what I think they must give political prisoners in war-torn countries, men with scraggly beards and dirt-crusty clothes crouching in cells wondering what happened to them. Jailers thrust buggy cups of water their way along with a little pile of matzoh and then slam the door on the prisoners. Swallow that. Goodbye. Slam. My dad has stalked off to read some newspapers in a lying-down position but I leave him alone and I stare at my binocular which has only a few bites out of it and the idea of touching it gives me a fluttery feeling within, like stealing or lying. I don't want to hurt my dad, who is not all that good at explaining stuff, my dad who is white hot I think, like the Sun, our nearest star, not blue hot like really big stars which burn ferocious and quick, something I read in one of Ben's books. After nearly billions of years, the Sun began to run out of hydrogen, its fuel, and some of its body, its elements, puffed away into space, but unlike the big fierce stars, it did not explode completely into little pulsing stars or faintly glowing clouds of stars. I don't know if I got this right, I can barely understand it, like trying to make out who it is coming toward you from across the street when you do not have your glasses on, but I think that maybe if you want to stay one big hot star, it is better to burn like the Sun, white hot, not blue hot. I think so.

Here is another time I asked my dad a religion question and I squeezed a few words out of him, some of his elements puffing away into my space. I am looking for shirt cardboard because I am doing a project and need to make a base for a battlefield. I will make trenches and broken trees and little mounds out of twigs and papier-mâché and stick it all on the shirt cardboard and paint it dirty green and brown and then put little soldiers in the battlefield. That's my plan. Okay. Dad is shaving in the big bathroom off his and Mum's bedroom. I know my dad is shaving because I can hear him breathing in and out in a grunty fashion all the way down the hall.

I knock on the open door.

"Dad?"

No Time

"I'm shaving!"

Do all guys shave like my dad? I won't know until I go out in the world and have a guy of my own, then I'll have a better idea if it's like this with all of them. I have a feeling it's not. My dad has no shirt on which is pretty wise, and his chin is way up in the air so I don't know how he can see what he is doing in the mirror. There are clumps of white cream all around the sink and both taps are running hard and he keeps slapping the razor against the rim of the sink everytime he finishes a stroke of it on his face where there are little blood specks near his nose. He is standing in water that has splashed at his feet like he is at the edge of the beach and the tide has just rolled up to him. It looks like a tough job. I speak to him from the doorway of the bathroom, and I don't get too close because my dad is not very good at remembering our ages and he may just slap some shaving cream on my face which is what he used to do when I was seven or so. I liked to watch him and would shave my cream off with a protractor from my geometry set, the best use I ever got out of a protractor. I am fourteen now, but my dad may not bear this in mind so I play it safe, out of reach.

"Dad? I need some shirt cardboard. Can I—may I look in your drawer?"

"Sure," my dad says, concentrating hard on shaving.

Someone else has been at the shirt cardboard because there are a lot of shirts in their plastic sleeves from the cleaner's but no cardboard. Harriet probably. Making something weird I bet. I have to search right to the bottom and I touch a tangly mess of belts. Not belts. It's like spaghetti of shiny black straps with squares of leather attached. It's in two parts. It looks like what they strap on victims in horror-type films before the mad doctor zaps them with electric charges for experimental purposes. Yikes.

My dad has finished shaving and comes into the bedroom for a shirt. He is like a soldier home from the front, a survivor. Well done, Dad.

"Outta my way!" he says, joking around tough.

I feel caught. My hands are in the spaghetti of straps so I have to ask him now, it's too late, my hands are in a frozen grip like I am doing something wrong. "Dad, what is this, what is it?"

"Ohhh," he says, letting out a big breath, the way he does when he has an important story to tell. "This belonged to my father."

"Okay," I say, meaning tell me more.

"These are phylacteries."

"Right. What do they do, Dad?"

My dad pulls out what looks like a tablecloth with a fringe. "It goes with this, a prayer shawl, see? Then you wrap this on one arm and the other bit around your head and that's it. It's for praying."

Very weird. "Cool," I say. "You don't use it?" I ask, a bit worried.

"No, Jem. I'm not Orthodox, I told you that."

"What are these boxes supposed to be?"

"It's the lost tribes, the lost tribes of Israel." My dad is losing interest, I can feel it, and it's not that he is drifting, but that I am, that maybe the force around him, his white heat not blue heat, this force of gravity I think, is pushing me away from him, like star mess, bits that come off in an explosion. Is this science? Is this a science thought? If it is, it is probably too girly to be right at all. I don't know if I should tell Ben my theory about Dad, I need to think it out first in case Ben gets more cross at me.

"What lost tribes, Dad, when, how did they get lost, where were they going?" How can a black leather box be a lost tribe, how?

"Jem. I have had a long day and have a headache. Now I am

going to have a drink with your mother in the kitchen. I have lots of books to show you. Maybe tomorrow. Ask me then, okay?"

My dad gets a lot of headaches and I hope when I grow up I will not be in a headache situation like my Dad and walk out on my kids in the middle of an explanation. That's an aim I have and I make a note of it.

"Put it away now, Jem. Be careful with it."

"Okay." These phylacteries don't look all that fragile to me. Never mind. If Dad says be careful, it means he has a big feeling for a thing, the way he does for books and that baseball he has with writing on it, some signature of a famous baseball player, etc. He doesn't have a lot of things and so you have to pay attention when he says be careful, and it makes you wonder about him, what is in his world, what things he has a big feeling for and why, like that painting Mum gave him of the boxer, Mr. Daniel Mendoza, a Jewish boxer, and a very famous one.

I fold the shawl. I try to compress the mess of straps in a neat way and tuck it back where it was. Phylacteries. I'm careful. I try to imagine my dad's father with a shawl and a yarmulke probably, a little hat my dad never lets me wear at Passover, never telling me why except to say, no Jem, no Jem, it's for boys, for men, no Jem, it's not for you. I imagine this man I never met, my grandfather, wearing these straps, doing some praying, and I wonder why I cannot feel a connection between that man and me, not a single thing, and it gives me a lonely feeling, like waiting at a bus stop with a friend and the bus suddenly comes and takes your friend away because you live in different places and need different buses. Dad said he was a junk dealer. What is that? I picture a dustman, riding the back of a rubbish truck, hanging on with one hand and smiling like you see some of them do, then jumping off and hauling up big dustbins. Was this my grandfather? Or did he sort through the rubbish, picking out the good bits and swapping it for other junk with other junk dealers, doing some junk dealing that is, a profession I have never heard of. I do not ask my dad because I feel like I should know what a junk dealer is, and that it is a bit sad to be one, and the way Dad said it, kind of cross and proud at the same time, "He was a junk dealer! A scrap man!" it was like the end of a conversation and not the start of one.

I wonder about praying too and how complicated it seems for everyone, such as nuns. Maybe a rosary is a bit like phylacteries, but at least it can pass for jewelry, whereas I can't imagine anyone wandering around with phylacteries on and not looking super-weird, like maybe seeing Marley's Ghost from *A Christmas Carol* right there in the open, in real life, walking along with the chain wrapped around him, the chain he forged in life as he puts it, the chain like a tail with those clanky metal objects connected to it, cashboxes, padlocks and purses and keys and so on, all these things being symbols of how Marley messed up in life. I've noticed that a lot of regular types, not just ghost or religious types, wear chains and bracelets and maybe all jewelry is symbolic, maybe. Mum has a cross which is not a cross, it is jewelry, she says, it is art. I don't know about this. It is a long and skinny silver crucifix with a moonstone at the heart of it where Jesus normally is. It is very beautiful, but she wears it under her clothes because she says Dad won't be very happy if she wears it on the outside. Okay.

At the convent, I sometimes go to assembly just to watch, although I am not supposed to go. My dad said, "Jem, I don't want you to go!" and gave me a dark look, like when he takes away your pocket money for some crime you did. When I do go to assembly, I watch the nuns and the girls making the sign of the cross, touching head and heart and shoulders and looking real glum and making prayers, some of them mixing all their fingers up and folding them down over the backs of their hands and a few of them placing palms together and pointing their fingers skyward, like in my favorite Renaissance paintings. I watch them all and wonder if you can't just be walking along and suddenly break into prayer inside your head, no speaking out loud, would it count, would the prayer make it to God without cross signs and prayer hands and speaking out loud, without rosaries and phylacteries and shawls and having to be in a special place? I think you should be able to do it this way, and if God is ALWAYS listening, etc., like the nuns tell you, making me think he is like Dr. Sigmund Freud in the documentary I saw, a man with a gray beard and specs sitting in an armchair and listening listening, and writing up all about the crazy types he.has been listening to, if God who = Jesus, also Jewish, just like Dr. Freud, if God is always listening, then I think he should be able to tell the difference between plain old talking to yourself inside your head and the prayer moment.

I have to stop thinking about God type stuff now due to getting a headache, making me worry that I am inheriting this from my dad too. I have to get back to science. I have to get unstuck from the past. I know one thing though, I don't want to ask M. Kassovitz a single question about religion. No.

M. Kassovitz is not an old science guy like they show you in scary films or comics or anything, he is not an old guy with crazy hair springing off his head, a wild determined look in his eyes behind thick specs, and a lot of layers of clothing that he hasn't washed in a long time, as if he could not get warm even in a country near the equator. Why are science guys made out to look crazy? Mme Beckers is not crazy or a guy. This scientist we all watch, the entire Weiss family sprawling around in front of the TV, enjoying free TV time, this man Carl Sagan is not wild at all. He is a star man, an astronomer, and he has a lot to say in a slightly spooky voice about space and other worlds, superspace and billions and billions of stars which is a phrase Gus and Harriet like to repeat in that spooky Carl Sagan voice, "Billions and BILLIONS of stars," they say, just like that out of nowhere and stare you right in the face until you feel the desire to bop them on the head with a rolled-up newspaper the way you train small puppies. In my experience, a puppy will do all the puppy stuff it needs to do anyway, never mind about the rolled-up newspaper you never really have the guts to whack him with, that puppy will chew all the legs of the kitchen chairs like they are corn on the cob, just leaving skinny cores of chewed-up wood, he will tear all the leather straps off your mum's shoes which will now be all streaked with dog drool plus eat her favorite pocket-sized book of poems and so on, he will do it all until it is just about time to stop being a puppy, and you have to hang in there and make a few sacrifices until he is ready to settle down a little and be a dog with decent manners. That's how it was with our Labrador baby dog and that's what I think about when Harriet and Gus come real close to me from behind a door or something and pop their eyes wide and tell me what's out there, "Billions and BILLIONS of stars."

When M. Kassovitz comes into our classroom for the first time and saunters up to the desk and lays his neat black briefcase on top of it, right away everyone feels bad. Everyone feels bad without knowing what we have done, all the girls look around at each other and we don't know what to do or say. M. Kassovitz has dark hair in tight curls and he wears specs that are a bit tinted, so you cannot see his eyes and he reads out all our names from a book, something none of our regular teachers do anymore and the nuns never do. He comes to my name which is right at the bottom before Younge, Margaret, who is a non-French kid like me, and he speaks it twice, "Weiss," he says. "Weiss."

"Here, Monsieur," I say and he takes a long look at me and that's where it all started, my really bad feeling for science and something else, too, something that makes me think about hand-to-hand combat in the First World War, out there in no-man's-land digging at a guy with a pointy bayonet and seeing him right close up, seeing he is just like you in most ways and feeling a bit silly because on Christmas Day you met in the middle and had schnapps with him and none of this seems right but you are pretty war-crazed and cannot think straight and make sensible decisions, especially in a hand-to-hand combat situation. That's how it is with M. Kassovitz, who is really mad at me, I think, because of my Jewish half and because I am at this convent where he thinks I should not be.

In history we are studying *les guerres de religion,* the Wars of Religion, 1562–1598. These were between Huguenots and Catholics, who are always picking on each other due to transubstantiation and other things, never settling down. M. Kassovitz and I are not so far apart either, but this is like a War of Religion, I think they all begin this way, with something small, like the name you have, and a stare held a little too long. I think so.

This is how else M. Kassovitz carries out this *guerre de religion* against his single enemy, me, Jemima Weiss. He makes me do all the physics problems he wants solved. He calls my name. He invites me to the blackboard. He knows I won't be able to do it and he watches me try until I don't try at all, I say I can't do it, I don't know how, please go away, someone send for Mme Beckers for whom I have a big feeling, someone send for her right now.

My dad has phylacteries, I want to tell him. At home, in the drawer, and a prayer shawl too. We celebrate Passover, a time when I do not get to wear a hat, and when I ask a lot of questions, inviting Jude to say, "What would you call this stage in your life, Jem? What would you call it? The incredibly annoying stage? The I never shut up stage? The stupid questions stage?" Jude butts me in the shoulder, like a lamb in a field.

And every Passover Harriet is a problem, big tears popping to the surface of her eyes and getting ready to roll out because she doesn't like to eat foodstuffs touching. "Not touching!" she cries. "Not touching!" My dad doesn't know how to handle this, he wants her to understand the symbol of things, he wants her to have matzoh and maror because of the bitterness of things for the Jews, he needs her to drop an egg in salty water to signify their tears and he is not good at explaining and is impatient to continue reading that book backwards, the Haggadah, and so Mum has to smile that smile of hers which is a special message for Harriet who comes back to us suddenly, reminding me of that experiment Mme Beckers explained, the one about displacement of water and how a thing takes up the space where something else was before, like with Harriet, how the crazy feeling makes way for the calm feeling, and I think how nothing is separate but works in a chain-like way, and I wonder where Harriet's crazy feeling went, maybe it went into me, maybe.

And now I don't want to tell any of this to M. Kassovitz. I know he will not think it is scientific. No. He wants me to explain this physics reaction he is demonstrating in our last physics class before the Christmas break. He stares at me where I am, in front of the class yet again, in a classroom where the mood is bad, like a lot of gas has escaped and is waiting to be lit in an explosion, and there I stand in my school uniform which suddenly feels cold and stiff like there is a drafty space between my skin and all the material that covers me.

M. Kassovitz drops a small pebble or something into a beaker filled with gassy water. It plunges to the bottom, then it rises to the surface, then falls again. It goes on and on. He waits for me to explain it and smiles a little and I hate him but I will not cry, no I will not and I want Ben here, Ben who is a magnet with special spook-power, I want Ben to tell me how to see this problem of rising and falling, rising and falling, how to take this stone in a beaker filled with bubbly liquid and fit it into the world where people are. I want Ben to tell me I can watch this experiment and get some science and travel around in time and get out of the past and connect things up, different times to different times, and us, Ben and me and every Weiss in all those times. I think about these things Ben promised me and I have no answer for M. Kassovitz, who sends me back to my seat like he is disgusted with me, like he is slamming the door on science, a place where I am not allowed, and this is pretty depressing. I sit down and I know suddenly he is not just my enemy but Ben's too, he is the opposite of Ben, he is a magnet that forces things away, something I remember Ben showing me once, talking about magnetic fields, turning a magnet to scatter and attract little iron filings, then placing two magnets together to demonstrate repulsion as he called it, placing them with their like poles facing north to north, south to south, giving me a strange sad feeling.

There was a lot of snow that Christmas, and some part of the way into our journey to the country house, with everyone piled on top of each other in the car, which was filled to the brim with Christmas stuff, our car like a Christmas stocking packed tight the way I love it, no room for even one more bitty chocolate, some part of the way there, the snow began to get all blowy and my dad hunched his shoulders and gripped the wheel in a cowboy-fierce grip, checking out the road ahead for icy patches just as if he were leading a wagon train of women and children through a dodgy mountain pass where Apaches lurk, bows drawn, ready to pierce us all with poisoned arrows.

The snow fell just about every day and night and I never get tired of snow. Harriet and I go out at night and flop backwards into fluffy heaps of it, the best type of bed you could dream of lying in, and we stare up at stars, our own private planetarium, and we gaze and gaze at them, a favorite activity of my little sister's. She points out that if you stare real hard, you will see more and more stars and twinkly streaks and maybe even some star motion, and I see what she means.

"Harriet?"

Harriet does not say "Yes?" or "What?" but she starts to giggle like she knows a joke is coming. She makes soft sneezy sounds and pats the snow with her white mittens that have little lamb faces on them, each hand looking like a little lamb mouth getting ready to go beh-beh-beh. Harriet opens and closes the lamb faces by slapping fingers against thumbs and she dips her hands in the ground, taking lamb bites of snow.

"Lambs get thirsty. Seven glasses of water a day," Harriet declares with authority. "That's what you need."

"I think it's six glasses, six is just fine and that's for humans, Harriet. People."

"Lambs need seven!"

"Okay, Harriet. But stop that now, your hands are going to be all freezing and you'll want to go in. Look up, look up."

Harriet folds her arms over her little chest and gazes skyward, looking like one of those stone tombs of medieval maidens, lovely wives of knights who died of broken hearts. Now that she is eleven, a stranger might think Harriet is getting a bit old for lamb mittens, lambs that need to drink snow to stay healthy, but I don't care, I don't think so, it's cool with me.

"Billions and BILLIONS of stars!" I say in Carl Sagan fashion and Harriet is laughing like crazy now, it doesn't take much sometimes to start her off and when Harriet laughs, not noisy but very determined, her whole body getting into it, she sticks with you no matter where you go until she has finished up laughing, like she really needs you to hear the whole thing, every single moment of her mirth, which is a word I like a lot. Even though pretty often I want to bop her on the head with a rolled-up newspaper, I decide that Harriet is my all-time favorite crazy person, that's what I decide. She is a star and she is crazy for stars.

Harriet = stardust.

Hey, Ghost. Can you—can you sit down? Ask him to sit down, Jem, and he'll bring all his friends. Do you have friends? I wear the chain. I don't know how to drive. Nearly Christmas again, twenty-one years on and I can't drive but I remember *la loi de Newton*, Newton's law, and I step on the brakes, that's what I do. Another star man, a science guy, writes these words. "In a sense, human flesh is made of stardust." Here's why, as far as I can tell. Before the Sun and the Earth were made, stars formed, got old and blew up in fierce explosions, scattering dust through space. The Sun was made from the primordial gas in our Galaxy, the Milky Way, which by then had enough heavy bits in it to make rocky planets like the Earth, and atoms escaped from these: carbon, nitrogen, oxygen, phosphorus, sulfur, calcium, sodium, potassium, iron, and all this made Harriet, her tissue, her teeth and little bones, her brain and her nerves, the color of her blood. The stars made the elements, they were not made in the Big Bang, the stars made them all except the lightest elements such as hydrogen, and an exploding star does what alchemy cannot, it reaches into the heart of things, the nucleus as it is called, and you have to get right in there to change the nature of a thing. Stars can fashion a new thing out of themselves the way alchemists could not wring gold from base metal, and this means there is a situation of nonstop creation and destruction out there in the Universe, and it also means maybe that a ghost is a shadow, the dust of something old with a suggestion of something new.

"Jude, you know why those are called tree-chocolates, you want to know why?" I ask him, not expecting an answer.

Jude is supervising the decoration of the Christmas tree, or Xmas tree, as Mum calls it so as to leave the Christ bit out, even though it means the same, due to X being the cross, the crucifix, but she says Xmas anyway so as not to upset my dad or something, a little bit like the way she wears a crucifix tucked under her clothes and says it is art, it is jewelry and not a cross. No one is hoodwinked around here. Never mind. Jude is supervising, which means he is lying on the sofa in front of the tree eating tree-chocolates, occasionally looping skinny little wires onto tree objects and passing them to us, but mainly telling us we are doing a real bad job and Mum won't like it. Thanks, Jude.

"Jude, they are called tree-chocolates," I explain, "because you put them up on the tree and then you take them off and eat them, everybody gets one. They are not sofa-chocolates. Get my 'rift?"

"Yeh-yeh," Jude says. "That side of the tree looks crap. Too much stuff and too much red, Mum's gonna hate that. 'Oh, darlings, what if?' That's what she'll say, in other words, start all over again, dumb-dumbs."

He's right. That's what she does. Mum will be called in by Ben to inspect the tree and we'll all know right away if it's no good because she'll say, "It's so lovely but, darlings, what if?" and pretty soon just about everything on the tree will move around or come off, mostly all the decorations that I put on but I don't care, although sometimes I think just Mum and Ben should do the tree due to their big thing for art. Harriet has a big thing for art but if you let her loose on the tree it will be covered in fauna and stars, the branches heaving under the weight of chocolate, her all-time favorite food group. It will be a crazy tree. Those are the facts.

Ben and I step back from the tree to get a better look and we climb backwards onto the sofa and stomp all over Jude as if we didn't know he was there, we trample him as much as possible saying, "Oops—sorry" quite a lot. It takes a while to get the tree done.

Gus is our lighting man, he works the lights even though he is only seven, but he has been studying Ben for at least three years, and Gus has a thing for electricity and machines of all kinds, I think he will be very good at science the way I am not, especially since M. Kassovitz and his *guerre de religion* against me. Gus may turn out to be a science guy himself and he will not be stuck in the past like his big sister Jem, no he won't.

If Mum comes in from the kitchen where she is deep into Christmas, I mean Xmas food preparations, if she passes through to check on us, we all stand around Gus so she can't see that he is testing the lights and this is due to her fear of fire. We all know Gus is okay, but it will be hard to explain this to Mum in a hurry and we are all pretty busy. It may be a Druid thing with her. This fear of fire is maybe a good witch thing, the opposite of what the wicked witch feels in *The Wizard of Oz*, for instance, the wicked witch having a big fear of water and perishing in a splash from a bucket, leaving behind only a screechy death whimper plus her pointy hat and broomstick in a puddle of H_2O which is the formula for water, one of about three things I can ever remember from chemistry.

Before I started messing up the tree with decorations, before Jude said it looks crap, Ben wound all the lights around the tree, leaving one little light at the top pointing skyward, the guiding starlight, and I like to watch Ben dance around the tree because he is so tall and when he is busy doing artistic activity, he is real graceful. Unlike Jude, he is too polite to tell me what I am doing is all wrong, but I notice that most times I turn and face up to the tree, the thing I have just attached is in some new better place. Okay.

It's a hard tree to decorate this year, it's all empty toward the top on one side like some bear took a bite out of it. My dad

brought it home, cutting it down with some of his drinking bud-
dies, two guys he met in a pub who paint houses and do carpentry
and so on. He is always meeting weird guys in pubs and Mum gets
a big heart for them, worrying they are lost souls and don't have all
the good things we are used to and pretty soon these guys are
hanging out in our house all the time like they are right in our
family. It's cool with us. But this is not a good tree, no.

"Well done, Gus," says Ben. "All the lights work."

Gus just tightens his lips and nods a few times, but we know he
is pleased.

"Hey, Gus, aren't you hot from doing the lights? You look hot,"
says Jude.

"Oh-oh," says Gus.

"Yeh, you look a bit steamed up," Ben says.

"Definitely," I add.

"Time to play 'Gus Go With Us,' " announces Jude and Gus
just giggles, standing there quivering but not running away. Gus
may have a big thing for science but he does not have a big thing
for escape, he is extremely good fun to torture and Jude and Ben
have an easy time of grabbing a wriggly Gus by his hands and feet
and tossing him into a snowbank and shutting the door on him.
When Gus makes it back in, he is still giggling to himself and
shaking snow off like a dog does.

"Hey, Gus," we say, real bored, like we had nothing to do with it.

My dad is loafing on the big sofa in a whole mess of newspapers
and he pays us no attention, doing his job of being the Sun our
nearest star, and all his kids revolving around him, little pulsing
stars maybe and making a lot of racket while he burns white hot,
not moving, just burning fierce.

"Dad? Were you drunk when you picked this tree?" I ask.

"What a way to talk to your father!" my dad says, not upset at all. "We made a few pit stops, sure."

"Because I don't call this a Christmas, oops, Xmas tree at all. It's a Christmas bush!" I tell him.

"A Christmas weed," says Jude.

"An idea of a tree," Ben adds. "An archetype of Tree!"

"That's what I get for marrying into a new-fangled religion," my dad says, stuffing newspapers onto the floor and rising up like a giant. "A bunch of tree-worshipers! White bread noshers! Knuckleheads! Jem! Sommelier! Go open champagne for your mother! Make tracks!"

I think about Saint Francis for a minute, a cool saint and the first stigmatist, and I remember how this whole Christmas business is because of him, how he set up little nativity scenes with Mary and her immaculate baby and Joseph and so on, kings and cows and lambs; I think how Francis even strung up lights just the way Gus and Ben have and how he did all this so the people would not be spooked by Jesus, how they would know he was a human with human ways. This is an olden times thought, I see that, but something about my dad always makes me do this, go right into the past looking for clues.

We all head for the kitchen, aiming to drink champagne which I will pour out, due to being tops at this job in the Weiss family, this job of sommelier as it is called, or sommelière if you are a girl, but my dad forgets this always, the girl version of the word. Never mind. We aim to hang out with Mum and Harriet for a while but when Ben and I reach the doorway we hear a thud of a noise, like snow falling off a roof and Ben knows right away what has happened.

"Oh no," says Ben and we both look back at the tree, our Xmas bush, our weedy archetype which has slumped over, falling on its face like a drunk.

"Ben," I say, kind of excited. "GRAVITY."

"Yup."

Ben and I head for the tree, we are determined but careful, on tiptoes just about, like stretcher-bearers rescuing a fallen man on a battlefield. I feel excited about the connection I made, I am on a science roll now, I am excited like I am winning a race I never thought I'd even be allowed to run.

"Gravity is the weakest of four forces in nature. Right, Ben?"

"Yup."

"It has to be weak enough for us to stand up and move around but strong enough to stop us getting ripped away into space, right?"

"Yup," says Ben.

"I don't get that part, the ripped away into space part. What happens then?"

Ben nearly has the tree up and I am fiddling around with bits of kindling and logs to wedge the trunk in the big brass bucket. I don't think this tree can take another fall, no.

"We might have to do this some other day, Jem, but you have to let go of this idea of one world. There is space and superspace, other worlds, sometimes just chaos-type universes, darkness, black holes and so on, but it's all out there and it is random, not absolute, you see?"

"No. What's that got to do with gravity, I said gravity and you said yup. Now I'm stuck again."

"It's just that there is old physics and quantum physics. There was Newton—"

"Newton! I know him! *La loi de Newton*, yeh!" I am flying again, racing.

Ben steps back to check out the Xmas bush. "Newton was wrong, Jem. Newton was wrong."

"No." I feel bad now, I don't know where this can lead and I sit down on Jude's sofa. Where is Jude? He's always there then not there and you don't know when it happened, the move he made. And where is Gus with the champagne?

"Where is Gus?" I say. "I poured that champagne about eighteen years ago. Get in here, Gus. Gus Come to Us!"

"You see? That's quantum physics."

"What is? Where?"

"Newton thought that gravity was a force on things and he thought time and space were absolute and you could measure them both at the same time and determine the outcome of things, like everything in the world is cause and effect, and that's not how it is. Time and space are not separate. It is spacetime, four dimensions, like that thing of Einstein's where he explains that at really high speeds, time slows down for the watching person, the train going by and the clock inside the train. I'll show you in my book but not tonight, okay? But you have to stop separating things. Light travels in waves and particles and it's different but it's one thing, like inside us there are electrons and subatomic particles and they are all in suspension, not separate things you can identify and they don't make a reality until you actually observe it, then it does what's called collapsing. It collapses into reality, your reality, the watcher's, which is one view of things, just one of many possible versions of it, right?"

"How can a thing be real and collapse? I don't get it and what's that got to do with Gus and champagne? Ben!" I am getting pan-icky now. I wish I'd never started this.

"Sorry. Okay, I mean it feels like eighteen years since you poured the champagne and Gus was supposed to bring the tray in but maybe for Gus it feels like just a few minutes . . . forget it, Jem, it's something about time being different for everyone, it's not ab-solute, Okay? You can't understand the Universe, you can't meas-ure everything at the same time, like speaking French and English at the same time, speed and movement are two different languages almost. That's all quantum theory stuff, the Uncertainty Principle it was called, about other worlds and reality being in your head, you made it yourself out of all the chaos, which is like raw material, see?"

"That's spooky, Ben. Like religion almost, not science at all."

"That's right!" says Ben, real pleased.

"It is? You'll have to explain again, maybe for eighteen years, okay? Not now though."

Here comes Gus.

"No problem," says Ben.

"Ben? I know one thing. Dad and Jude are very sensitive to gravity, the weakest force, because they are always lying around on sofas and standing up is quite hard for them. How about that?"

"Jem, you're getting really good at this. You are tops at science. Tops." Ben pats me hard on the head with his big hand with the long graceful fingers and I fall on the ground in a heap.

"I'm collapsing into a reality heap, Ben."

"Yup," he says, taking a handful of nuts and raisins from a bowl on the table I get busy clearing so Gus can lay the tray down, a tray with seven flûtes and a bottle of champagne on it which Gus carries, no problem, even though he is only a little kid still. Gus is a bit like Mum when it comes to movement, he glides around like a hart or something, a Renaissance-painting type beast, not capable of a single ugly move, not even when taken by surprise.

The room is filling up with all the Weisses and I can see them and feel them, the room is now a different place, all charged up with something and maybe this is reality collapsing, I'm not sure. I think how I am getting ready to give up on science and stay in the past where maybe I belong, like my dad, I think how science is just too hard for me, it makes me sad because I cannot fit it into the world but it could be that is the way with science, that you can grasp one bare idea like gravity and the moment you do that, lots of other problems rise up that you never expected, like Ben talking about light traveling two different ways, two different ways you cannot separate, and I can't understand this, how can light travel, how does a thing you cannot see move around, like a ghost, how? And this is my problem with science, that I need to see and feel it. I need to see and feel it the way I do my family filling up the room just now with their electrons and subatomic particles and so on.

I may have to tell Ben that he must give up on me in a science situation, but I don't want to let him down and also I love to listen to him, I love it even if I cannot understand and maybe this is one way to have a big thing for Ben, maybe this is how he collapses for me, this is my possible world of Ben, but that's not science, Jem, no I don't think so.

There is Jude and he has handed out flûtes of champagne, joy juice my dad calls it, due to the effect it has on Mum. Jude passes out the glasses and he cracks jokes in a mumbly voice and he is not in a hurry, not ever, but everyone has champagne now, even Harriet with her little thimbleful she holds like it is a magic potion, nips of wine not enough for a small bird. Why is it Jude does things in no time at all it seems and yet not quick, but at thought-speed, Jude-speed? Maybe it is what Ben meant about speed and motion, that you cannot measure them at the same time, they are together and apart, two languages.

Ben drops a raisin in Gus's glass, he does it accidentally on purpose and I cannot believe my eyes because it is M. Kassovitz's experiment, the one he used in his *guerre de religion* against me, the raisin is rising and falling in the tall skinny glass and Gus smiles at it.

"Gus! Look at that!" I say, and then Gus, who is only seven and has a way with electricity, explains it to me real calm, he tells me why it is happening, that little bubbles cling to the raisin and lift it to the surface where the gas escapes, letting the raisin sink again, nothing to help it upward, and Gus is not at all surprised this knowledge is so easy for him and I know now I have to let go of science, I have to leave it to Gus.

Harriet says, "I'm drunk. Mummy. Harriet is drunk."

"I know a good cure for that," Jude says, getting ready to pitch Harriet into the snow.

"No! No!" screams my sister, flapping her wings now like a small bird jostled in a tight squeeze of a nest by another bird. "Harriet's okay."

I drink champagne and I think I can see it, light traveling in waves and particles, moving around and through Mum and my dad, around Ben and Jude and through Harriet and Gus, Gus most of all, Gus who has a way with light. I am in spacetime, I want to tell Ben that, and inside me is chaos I think, everything suspended although I can feel all the particles and atoms now, everything rising and falling, rising and falling within, a feeling that is spooky and good at the same time, the way feelings are that come in a rush and are maybe important but you don't know why, and I remember Mme Beckers teaching displacement and it could be that, each Weiss shifting and traveling, entering and leaving every other Weiss in the room, seven worlds all mixing up, but whatever it is, I hold still for it. I keep still for the light show.

I am crazy for this business of light, that it will do what it will do, that it needs no one, no divine management, its nature determining its behavior, and that it chooses the briefest path although the briefest path is not always the straightest. Light is smart, it is bright, it finds the briefest path by testing out all possible paths, traveling in waves and particles, roaming every which way until it finds the right one and you don't see all the mistakes. And so I know you, Ghost. Stop shimmying and sit down; you don't fox me. Reflection. Rebounding of a wave of light or other radiation when it strikes a surface. Spirit in the mirror, settle down. Brakes on. You are me. You wear the chain I forged in life, electrons, stardust, shadow and projection, a message out of the past into the now, stigmata like the four fibroids on my womb, I think, my benign tumors. I love this word benign, I picture a drunken friend, funny and loose-limbed, his worst offense too many words, his darkest crime to make you worry and help him home; he is benign.

I am all science now too, you can all take me apart, step right up, here is my body, here is my blood, what can you tell me, and I like this new doctor, she comes from a war-torn country, all good doctors come from war-torn countries, I think so. She is gentle and calm and rests against the frame of the cubicle as I haul my jeans over my tight web of lean tissue and muscle, covering up for chaos within. Cover for me, cover me. She says I may not have children and I think but I have children, I've had children. Mary Immaculate. My four fibroids are of different lengths and sizes and they are benign, and I name them, Ben, Jude, Harriet, Gus. Stigmata. I wear the chain.

Christmas Eve, again, again and I have a thought for Saint Francis, the first stigmatist, who also had a big thing for Christmas and I step on the brakes, I stop hurtling through space, I turn fear into adrenaline and I travel in time, maybe not the way Ben wanted me to, but then I don't understand science, and on this night, with all the Weisses far apart but inseparable and in suspension, I do it, I collapse you all in no time.

Einstein explained how motion affects time and space, how they are not absolute, Newton was wrong. In Einstein's train story, a watcher is on the bank and a train whizzes past, a locomotive with a man inside, and a clock, and the way he sees it from the bank, that man's heartbeat slows, and his biological growth, and the clock slows too. Here's what I do, I load you on a train, Mum, Dad, Ben, Jude, Harriet, Gus, make tracks! And I have to stay behind, I cannot ride with you and I need this train to go fast, four-fifths the speed of light will do. Just let me watch.

ABOUT THE AUTHOR

Emma Richler was born in London and grew up there
and in Montreal. She read French literature at the University
of Toronto and the Université de Provence, before
training as an actress at the Circle in the Square in
New York City and working for ten years in the UK in
theatre, film, television drama and on BBC radio. She
lives in London.